P9-BZS-436

The Author

STEPHEN LEACOCK was born in Swanmore, Hampshire, England, in 1869. His family emigrated to Canada in 1876 and settled on a farm north of Toronto. Educated at Upper Canada College and the University of Toronto, Leacock pursued graduate studies in economics at the University of Chicago, where he studied under Thorstein Veblen.

Even before he completed his doctorate, Leacock accepted a position as sessional lecturer in political science and economics at McGill University. When he received his Ph.D. in 1903, he was appointed to the full position of lecturer. From 1908 until his retirement in 1936, he chaired the Department of Political Science and Economics.

Leacock's most profitable book was his textbook, *Elements of Political Science*, which was translated into seventeen languages. The author of nineteen books and countless articles on economics, history, and political science, Leacock turned to the writing of humour as his beloved avocation. His first collection of comic stories, *Literary Lapses*, appeared in 1910, and from that time until his death he published a volume of humour almost every year.

Leacock also wrote popular biographies of his two favourite writers, Mark Twain and Charles Dickens. At the time of his death, he left four completed chapters of what was to have been his autobiography. These were published posthumously under the title *The Boy I Left Behind Me*.

Stephen Leacock died in Toronto, Ontario, in 1944.

THE NEW CANADIAN LIBRARY

General Editor: David Staines

ADVISORY BOARD
Alice Munro
W.H. New
Guy Vanderhaeghe

STEPHEN LEACOCK

My Remarkable Uncle

and Other Sketches

With an Afterword by Barbara Nimmo

Copyright © 1942 by Dodd, Mead and Company Inc.
Afterword copyright © 1989 by Barbara Nimmo

Reprinted 1989

All rights reserved. The use of any part of this publication reproduced, transmitted in any form or by any means, electronic, mechanical, photocopying, recording, or otherwise, or stored in a retrieval system, without the prior consent of the publisher is an infringement of the copyright law.

Canadian Cataloguing in Publication Data

Leacock, Stephen, 1869–1944
My remarkable uncle

(New Canadian Library)
Bibliography: p.
ISBN 0-7710-9965-7

I. Title. II. Series.

PS8523.E15M9 1989 C813'.52 C88-094967-8
PR9199.2.L42M9 1989

Typesetting by Pickwick

Printed and bound in Canada

McClelland & Stewart Inc.
The Canadian Publishers
481 University Avenue
Toronto, Ontario
M5G 2E9

Contents

Some Memories

My Remarkable Uncle

A Personal Document

THE MOST remarkable man I have ever known in my life was my uncle Edward Philip Leacock – known to ever so many people in Winnipeg fifty or sixty years ago as E.P. His character was so exceptional that it needs nothing but plain narration. It was so exaggerated already that you couldn't exaggerate it.

When I was a boy of six, my father brought us, a family flock, to settle on an Ontario farm. We lived in an isolation unknown, in these days of radio, anywhere in the world. We were thirty-five miles from a railway. There were no newspapers. Nobody came and went. There was nowhere to come and go. In the solitude of the dark winter nights the stillness was that of eternity.

Into this isolation there broke, two years later, my dynamic Uncle Edward, my father's younger brother. He had just come from a year's travel around the Mediterranean. He must have been about twenty-eight, but seemed a more than adult man, bronzed and self-confident, with a square beard like a Plantagenet King. His talk was of Algiers, of the African slave market; of the Golden Horn and the Pyramids. To us it sounded like the *Arabian Nights*. When we asked, "Uncle Edward, do you know the Prince of Wales?" he answered, "Quite intimately" –

with no further explanation. It was an impressive trick he had.

In that year, 1878, there was a general election in Canada. E.P. was in it up to the neck in less than no time. He picked up the history and politics of Upper Canada in a day, and in a week knew everybody in the countryside. He spoke at every meeting, but his strong point was the personal contact of electioneering, of bar-room treats. This gave full scope for his marvellous talent for flattery and make-believe.

"Why, let me see" – he would say to some tattered country specimen beside him glass in hand – "surely, if your name is Framley, you must be a relation of my dear old friend General Sir Charles Framley of the Horse Artillery?" "Mebbe," the flattered specimen would answer. "I guess, mebbe; I ain't kept track very good of my folks in the old country." "Dear me! I must tell Sir Charles that I've seen you. He'll be so pleased." . . . In this way in a fortnight E.P. had conferred honours and distinctions on half the township of Georgina. They lived in a recaptured atmosphere of generals, admirals and earls. Vote? How else could they vote than conservative, men of family like them?

It goes without saying that in politics, then and always, E.P. was on the conservative, the *aristocratic* side, but along with that was hail-fellow-well-met with the humblest. This was instinct. A democrat can't condescend. He's down already. But when a conservative stoops, he conquers.

The election, of course, was a walk-over. E.P. might have stayed to reap the fruits. But he knew better. Ontario at that day was too small a horizon. For these were the days of the hard times of Ontario farming, when mortgages fell like snowflakes, and farmers were sold up, or sold out, or went "to the States," or faded humbly underground.

But all the talk was of Manitoba now opening up. Nothing would do E.P. but that he and my father must go west. So we had a sale of our farm, with refreshments, old-time fashion, for the buyers. The poor, lean cattle and the broken machines fetched less than the price of the whisky. But E.P. laughed it all off, quoted that the star of the Empire glittered in the west, and off to the West they went, leaving us children behind at school.

They hit Winnipeg just on the rise of the boom, and E.P. came at once into his own and rode on the crest of the wave. There is something of magic appeal in the rush and movement of a "boom" town – a Winnipeg of the 80's, a Carson City of the 60's. . . . Life comes to a focus; it is all here and now, all *present*, no past and no outside – just a clatter of hammers and saws, rounds of drinks and rolls of money. In such an atmosphere every man seems a remarkable fellow, a man of exception; individuality separates out and character blossoms like a rose.

E.P. came into his own. In less than no time he was in everything and knew everybody, conferring titles and honours up and down Portage Avenue. In six months he had a great fortune, on paper; took a trip east and brought back a charming wife from Toronto; built a large house beside the river; filled it with pictures that he said were his ancestors, and carried on in it a roaring hospitality that never stopped.

His activities were wide. He was president of a bank (that never opened), head of a brewery (for brewing the Red River) and, above all, secretary-treasurer of the Winnipeg Hudson Bay and Arctic Ocean Railway that had a charter authorizing it to build a road to the Arctic Ocean, when it got ready. They had no track, but they printed stationery and passes, and in return E.P. received passes over all North America.

But naturally his main hold was politics. He was elected right away into the Manitoba Legislature. They would have made him Prime Minister but for the existence of the grand old man of the province, John Norquay. But even at that in a very short time Norquay ate out of E.P.'s hand, and E.P. led him on a string. I remember how they came down to Toronto, when I was a schoolboy, with an adherent group of "Westerners," all in heavy buffalo coats and bearded like Assyrians. E.P. paraded them on King Street like a returned explorer with savages.

Naturally E.P.'s politics remained conservative. But he pitched the note higher. Even the ancestors weren't good enough. He invented a Portuguese Dukedom (some one of our family once worked in Portugal) – and he conferred it, by some kind of reversion, on my elder brother Jim who had gone to Winnipeg to work in E.P.'s office. This enabled him to say to visitors in his big house, after looking at the ancestors – to say in a half-whisper behind his hand, "Strange to think that two deaths would make that boy a Portuguese Duke." But Jim never knew which two Portuguese to kill.

To aristocracy E.P. also added a touch of peculiar prestige by always being apparently just about to be called away – imperially. If some one said, "Will you be in Winnipeg all winter, Mr. Leacock?" he answered, "It will depend a good deal on what happens in West Africa." Just that; West Africa beat them.

Then came the crash of the Manitoba boom. Simple people, like my father, were wiped out in a day. Not so E.P. The crash just gave him a lift as the smash of a big wave lifts a strong swimmer. He just went right on. I believe that in reality he was left utterly bankrupt. But it made no difference. He used credit instead of cash. He still had his imaginary bank, and his railway to the Arctic Ocean. Hospitality still roared and the tradesmen still paid for it. Any one who called about a bill was told that E.P.'s movements were uncertain and would depend a good deal on what happened in Johannesburg. That held them another six months.

It was during this period that I used to see him when he made his periodic trips "east," to impress his creditors in the West. He floated, at first very easily, on hotel credit, borrowed loans and unpaid bills. A banker, especially a country town banker, was his natural mark and victim. He would tremble as E.P. came in, like a stock-dove that sees a hawk. E.P.'s method was so simple; it was like showing a farmer peas under thimbles. As he entered the banker's side-office he would say: "I say. Do you fish? Surely that's a greenhart casting-rod on the wall?" (E.P. knew the names of everything.) In a few minutes the banker, flushed and pleased, was exhibiting the rod, and showing flies in a box out of a drawer. When E.P. went out he carried a hundred dollars with him. There was no security. The transaction was all over.

He dealt similarly with credit, with hotels, livery stables and bills in shops. They all fell for his method. He bought with lavish generosity, never asking a price. He never suggested pay till just as an afterthought, just as he was going out. And then: "By the way, please let me have the account promptly. I may be going away," and, in an aside to me, as if not meant for the shop, "Sir Henry Loch has cabled again from West Africa." And so out; they had never seen him before; nor since.

The proceeding with a hotel was different. A country hotel was, of course, easy, in fact too easy. E.P. would sometimes pay such a bill in cash, just as a sportsman won't shoot a sitting partridge. But a large hotel was another thing. E.P., on leaving – that is, when all ready to leave, coat, bag and all – would call for his bill at the desk. At the sight of it he would break out into enthusiasm at the reasonableness of it. "Just think!" he would say in his "aside" to me, "compare that with the Hotel Crillon in Paris!" The hotel proprietor had no way of doing this; he just felt that he ran a cheap hotel. Then another "aside," "Do remind me to mention to Sir John how admirably we've been treated; he's coming here next week." "Sir John" was our Prime Minister and the hotel keeper hadn't known he was coming – and he wasn't. . . . Then came the final touch – "Now, let me see . . . seventy-six dollars . . . seventy-six. . . . You give me" – and E.P. fixed his eye firmly on the hotel man – "give me twenty-four dollars, and then I can remember to send an even hundred." The man's hand trembled. But he gave it.

This does not mean that E.P. was in any sense a crook, in any degree dishonest. His bills to him were just "deferred pay," like the British debts to the United States. He never did, never contemplated, a crooked deal in his life. All his grand schemes were as open as sunlight – and as empty.

In all his interviews E.P. could fashion his talk to his audience. On one of his appearances I introduced him to a group of college friends, young men near to degrees, to whom degrees mean everything. In casual conversation E.P. turned to me and said, "Oh, by the way you'll be glad to know that I've just received my honorary degree from the Vatican – at last!" The "at last" was a knock-out – a degree from the Pope, and overdue at that!

Of course it could not last. Gradually credit crumbles. Faith weakens. Creditors grow hard, and friends turn their faces away. Gradually E.P. sank down. The death of his wife had left him a widower, a shuffling, half-shabby figure, familiar on the street, that would have been pathetic but for his indomitable self-belief, the illumination of his mind. Even at that, times grew hard with him. At length even the simple credit of the bar-rooms broke under him. I have been told by my brother Jim – the Portuguese Duke – of E.P. being put out of a Winnipeg bar, by an angry bartender who at last broke the mesmerism. E.P. had brought in a little group, spread up the fingers of one hand and said, "Mr. Leacock, five!" . . . The bar-tender broke into oaths. E.P. hooked a friend by the arm. "Come away," he said. "I'm afraid the poor fellow's crazy! But I hate to report him."

Presently even his power to travel came to an end. The railways found out at last that there wasn't any Arctic Ocean, and anyway the printer wouldn't print.

Just once again he managed to "come east." It was in June 1891. I met him forging along King Street in Toronto – a trifle shabby but with a plug hat with a big band of crape round it. "Poor Sir John," he said. "I felt I simply must come down for his funeral." Then I remembered that the Prime Minister was dead, and realized that kindly sentiment had meant free transportation.

That was the last I ever saw of E.P. A little after that some one paid his fare back to England. He received, from some family trust, a little income of perhaps two pounds a week. On that he lived, with such dignity as might be, in a lost village in Worcestershire. He told the people of the village – so I learned later – that his stay was uncertain; it would depend a good deal on what happened in China. But nothing happened in China; there he stayed, years and years. There he might have finished out, but for a strange chance of fortune, a sort of poetic justice, that gave E.P. an evening in the sunset.

It happened that in the part of England where our family belonged there was an ancient religious brotherhood, with a monastery and dilapidated estates that went back for centuries. E.P. descended on them, the brothers seeming to him an easy mark, as brothers indeed are. In the course of his pious "retreat," E.P. took a look into the brothers' finances, and his quick intelligence discovered an old claim against the British Government, large in amount and valid beyond a doubt.

In less than no time E.P. was at Westminster, representing the brothers. He knew exactly how to handle British officials; they were easier even than Ontario hotel keepers. All that is needed is hints of marvellous investment overseas. They never go there but they remember how they just missed Johannesburg or were just late on Persian oil. All E.P. needed was his Arctic Railway. "When you come out, I must take you over our railway. I really think that as soon as we reached the Coppermine River we must put the shares on here; it's too big for New York. . . ."

So E.P. got what he wanted. The British Government are so used to old claims that it would as soon pay as not. There are plenty left.

The brothers got a whole lot of money. In gratitude they invited E.P. to be their permanent manager; so there he was, lifted into ease and affluence. The years went easily by, among gardens, orchards and fishponds old as the Crusades.

When I was lecturing in London in 1921 he wrote to me: "Do come down; I am too old now to travel; but any day you like I will send a chauffeur with a car and two lay-brothers to bring you down." I thought the "lay-brothers" a fine touch – just like E.P.

I couldn't go. I never saw him again. He ended out his days at the monastery, no cable calling him to West Africa. Years ago I used to think of E.P. as a sort of humbug, a source of humour. Looking back now I realize better the unbeatable quality of his spirit, the mark, we like to think just now, of the British race.

If there is a paradise, I am sure he will get in. He will say at the gate – "Peter? Then surely you must be a relation of Lord Peter of Tichfield?"

But if he fails, then, as the Spaniards say so fittingly, "May the earth lie light upon him."

The Old Farm and the New Frame

When I left the old farm of my childhood which I described in talking about my remarkable uncle, I never saw it again for years and years. I don't think I wanted to. Most people who come off farms never go back. They talk about it, cry about it – but they don't really go. They know better.

If they did go back, they would find, as I did, the old place all changed, the old world all gone, in fact no "farms" any more, no cross-road stores, no villages – nothing in the old sense. A new world has replaced it all.

I went back the other day in a motor car to have a look round the locality that I hadn't seen since I left it by means of a horse and buggy more than half a century before. I came to do this because I happened to have been looking at one of those typical "motor ads" that you see in the coloured illustrations, motors glistening to an impossible effulgence, a gravelled drive impossibly neat, beside wide lawns of inconceivable grass and unachievable flower beds. In and beside the motor car were super-world beings as impossible as the grass and flowers around them – youths as square in the shoulders as Greek gods, girls as golden as guineas, and even old age, in the persons of the senior generation, smoothed and beautified to a pink and white as immaculate as youth itself. And as I looked at the picture of this transformed world not yet achieved but at least existing, in the creative mind of the artist, I fell to thinking of all the actual transformation that new invention has brought into our lives.

I thought particularly of how it has changed the aspect of what we used to call the country – the country of the horse and buggy days that I so easily recall. So I went back.

Our farm was up in a lost corner of Ontario, but the locality doesn't particularly matter. They're all the same from Ontario to Ohio.

We lived four and a half miles from "the village." To get to it from our farm you went down a lane – heavy going – up to the hubs in bad weather, then on to a road and up a hill, the same hill really you had just come down only on a different angle; then along a splendid "spin" of at least three hundred yards where you "let the mare out," that is, made her go like blazes (eight miles an hour); then, Whoa! steady! another hill, a mighty steep one, to go down. You had to take it pretty easy. In fact, for the hills you had far better get out and walk, as we generally did; it eased the mare to have us walk up the first hill and it eased the buggy to have us walk down the second.

After the second hill, a fine spin of about four hundred yards, good road and "room to pass." You couldn't "let the mare out" all along this, as it might "wind" her; but she could keep going at a pretty smart clip just the same. Then came the "big swamp," about three quarters of a mile or more, in fact. I never knew a road from Maine to the Mississippi that didn't have a swamp in it. A lot of the big swamp was "corduroy" road. The word means *corde du roi*, or king's rope, but the thing meant logs laid side by side with dirt shoveled over them. In the swamp there was no room to pass except by a feat of engineering in chosen spots.

After the swamp you went on over a succession of "spins" and "hills," the mare alternately "eased" and "winded" and "let out" – and at last, there you were, in the village street – yes, sir, right in the village, under an hour, pretty good going, eh? Cover the mare up with a blanket while we go into the tavern or she may get the "heaves" – or the "humps" – or I forget what; anyway it was what a mare got if you stayed too long in the tavern.

And the village street, how well I remember it! Romantic, well, I don't know; I suppose it was. But it was just a street – stores on each side with a square sign over each. Trees here and there. Horses hitched to posts asleep; a grist mill at the end where the river hit the village or the village hit the river, I forget which. There were no fancy signs, no fancy stores. The sole place of entertainment was the tavern – beer 5 cents, whisky 5 cents, mixed drinks (that means beer with whisky or whisky mixed with beer) 5 cents. Food, only at meal times, at a York shilling a meal, later raised to a quarter.

Such was the typical farm road and village of fifty years ago – a "social cell" as I believe the sociologists would call us.

Now look at the change. I visited it, as I say, the other day in a large smooth-running motor car – this "social cell" from which I emerged fifty years ago. Changed? The word isn't adequate. It just wasn't there any more. In the first place some one had changed our old farm-house into a "farmstead." You see, you can't live any longer on a farm if you are going to have people coming to see you in motor cars – golden girls, Apollo boys and Joan and Darby elders. You must turn the place into a "farmstead" – with big shingles all over it in all directions – with a "loggia" in front and a "pergola" at the side.

And the road? All gone, all changed. A great highway swept by in its course and sheared lane and hills into one broad, flat curve; threw aside the second hill into a mere nothing of a "grade," with a row of white posts; and the swamp, it has passed out of existence to become a broad flat with a boulevarded two-way road, set with new shingled bungalows with loggias and pergolas, over-grown with wistaria and perugia, and all trying to live up to the passing motor cars. There's a tea room now where the spring used to be, in the center of the swamp, the place where we watered the mare to prevent her blowing.

But you hardly see all this – the whole transit from farmstead to village by the sweeping, shortened concrete road is just three minutes. You are in the village before you know it.

And the village itself! Why, it's another place. What charm is this, what magic this transformation? I hardly know the place; in fact, I don't know it. The whole length of it now is neat with clipped grass and the next-to-impossible flowers copied from the motor car advertisements; there are trim little cedars and box hedges, trees clipped to a Versailles perfection and house fronts all aglow with variegated paint and hanging flowers. . . . And the signs, what a multitude of them; it's like a mediaeval fair! "Old English Tea Room"! I didn't know this was England! And no, it isn't; see the next sign, "Old Dutch Tea Room," and "Old Colony Rest House"! and "Normandy Post House"! No, it's not England; I don't know where it is.

But those signs are only a fraction of the total, each one vying with the last in the art of its decoration or the angle of its suspension. "Joe's Garage"! Look at it – built like a little Tudor house, half-timbered in black and white. Joe's grandfather was the village blacksmith, I remember him well, and his "blacksmith shop" was a crazy sort of wooden shed, out of slope, with no front side in particular and a forge in it. If they had it now they would label it "Ye Olde Forge" and make it an out-of-town eating place.

But these new signs mean that, for the people who ride from the city, in the motor cars, the village and its little river has become a "fishing resort." You see, it's only fifty-six miles from the city; you run out in an hour or so. You can rent a punt for $1 and a man to go with you and row for another $1 – or he'll fish for you, if you like. Bait only costs about 50 cents and you can get a fine chicken dinner, wine and all, from about $2. In short, you have a wonderful time and only spend $10; yet when I was young if you had $10 in the village no one could change it, and $10 would board you for a month.

And the people too! A new kind of people seems to have come into – or, no, grown up in – the village. I find, on examination, that they're really the grandsons and granddaughters of the people who were there. But the new world has taken hold of them and turned them into a new and different sort of people – into super people as it were.

Joe Hayes for example – you remember his grandfather, the blacksmith – has turned into a "garage man," handy, efficient, knowing more than a science college, a friend in distress. What the horse-and-buggy doctor of the countryside was to the sick of fifty years ago, such is now the garage man to the disabled motor car and its occupants towed into his orbit. People talk now of their mimic roadside adventures and tell how there "wasn't a garage man within five miles" as people used to tell of having to fetch the doctor at night over five miles of mud and corduroy.

And Joe's brothers and cousins have somehow turned into motor-men of all sorts, taximen, and even that higher race, the truckmen. What the "draymen" of Old London were, admired for their bulk and strength even by the fairest of the ladies, so today are the "truckmen" who have stepped into their place in evolution. . . .

Nor is it one sex only that the motor has transformed. People who live in a village where motors come and go must needs take thought for their appearance. See that sign BEAUTY PARLOR! You'd hardly think that that means Phoebe Crawford, whose great-aunt was the village seamstress. Or that other sign, GEORGETTE: LINGERIE, that's Mary Ann Crowder. Her grandfather was Old Man Crowder up the river.

Changed, isn't it? Wonderfully changed, into a sort of prettier and brighter world. And if a little "social cell" has changed like this, it's only part of the transformation that has redecorated all our world.

The only trouble is to live up to it – to be as neat and

beautiful as a beauty parlor girl, as friendly as a garage man, as bold and brave as a truck driver and as fit guest to sit down to a frogs' legs dinner in an Old Mill chophouse.

Alas! This happy world that might have been, that seemed about to be! The transformation from the grim and somber country-side to all this light and colour, had it only just begun to be overwhelmed and lost in the shadow of the War?

Perhaps the old farm had something to it after all.

The Struggle to Make Us Gentlemen

(A Memory of My Old School)

I MENTIONED above that I had gone away from the farm where I lived as a child to a boarding-school – the old Upper Canada College that stood half a century ago on King Street in Toronto. It has all been knocked down since. I look back at it now with that peculiar affection that every one feels for his old school after it has been knocked down and all the masters dead long ago.

But certain things that I was reading the other day, in the English papers, brought the old school back vividly to my mind. What I was reading belonged in the present English discussion, which the war had so much accentuated, about social classes, and whether "gentlemen" can go on finding a place. For it seems there is a good deal of alarm now in England over the idea that "gentlemen" may be dying out. In an old civilization things come and go. Knighthood came and went; it was in the flower, then in the pod and then all went to seed. Now it seems to be gentlemen that are going. It appears that the upper classes are being so depressed and the lower classes so pushed up, and both shifting sideways so fast, that you simply can't distinguish an upper birth from a lower. In fact it is hard to make up their births at all.

I wasn't meaning to write on that topic. The thing is too big. Every one admits that if gentlemen go, then Heaven only knows what will happen to England. But then Heaven only ever did. But the point here is that the question has got mixed up with the fate of the public schools; I mean of course public in the English sense, the ones the public can't get into. The best solution – it is generally admitted – in fact a solution "definitely in sight" is in the idea that if you throw the big board schools into the public schools and then throw the small private schools into both of them, then you so mix up your gentlemen with your others that they all turn into gentlemen. Of course you can't face this all at once; a whole nation of gentlemen is a goal rather than – well, I mean to say it takes time. Meantime, if it is "definitely in sight," that's the place where the genius of England likes to leave it. It can roost there and go fast asleep along with Dominion Status for India and the Disestablishment of the Church.

So, as I say, this talk of "gentlemen" in England turned me back to our Upper Canada College on King Street sixty years ago, and the desperate struggle there to make us gentlemen. We didn't understand for a while just what they were trying to do to us. But gradually we began to catch on to it, and feel that it was no good. There was a kindly and oratorical principal, whom I will not name but whom the affection of Old Boys will easily recall – a kindly principal, I say, with a beautiful and sonorous voice that used to echo through the Prayer Hall in exaltation of the topic. "This school, I insist," he would declaim, "must be a school of *gentlemen*." We used to sit as juniors and think: "Gee! This is going to be a tight shave! I'll never make it." But presently we learned to take it more easily. We noticed that the gentlemen question broke out after a theft of school-books, or the disappearance of small change foolishly left in reach. Not being yet gentlemen, we made a distinction between "stealing" a thing and "hooking" it. A gentleman, you see, classes both together. He'd just as soon steal a thing as hook it.

But, bit by bit and gradually, we were led towards the ideal. We were often told, by oratorical visitors, that Upper Canada College was founded as a "school for gentlemen." When I entered the school there were still a few old, very old, boys around, who belonged to the early generations of the foundation. We felt that the school had been fooled in some of them. They seemed just like us.

Personally, however, I got by on a side issue. In those days there was none of the elaborate registration, the card index stuff, that all schools have now. Any information that they wanted about us they got *viva voce* on the spot by calling us up in front of the class and asking for it. So there came a day soon after I entered when the principal called me up to be questioned and a junior master wrote down the answers. "What," he asked, "is your father's occupation?" I hesitated quite a while and then I said, "He doesn't do anything." The principal bent over towards the junior master who was writing and said in an impressive voice, "A gentleman." A sort of awe spread round the room at my high status. But really why I had hesitated was because I didn't know what to say. You see, I knew that my father, when in Toronto, was probably to be found along on King Street having a Tom-and-Jerry in the Dog and Duck, or at Clancy's – but whether to call that his occupation was a nice question.

Slowly we learned the qualifications of a gentleman and saw that the thing was hopeless. A gentleman it seemed would take a bath (once a week on bath night) and never try to dodge it. A gentleman would not chew gum in St. George's Church, nor imitate the voice of an Anglican Bishop. A gentleman, it seemed, *couldn't* tell a lie – not wouldn't, just couldn't. Limitations like these cut such a swath through our numbers that in time we simply gave up. There was no use in it. Mind, don't misunderstand me. Of course we could behave like gentlemen – oh, certainly – *act* like gentlemen. At first sight you'd mistake us for it. But we knew all the time that we weren't.

So, like the other boys, I left school still puzzled about the gentlemen business, and as the years have gone by the perplexity has only gone deeper. What is, or was, a gentleman, anyway? I remember that a little after I left school, while I was at college, there was a famous Canadian murder case that attracted wide attention because the murderer, who was presently hanged, was a gentleman. He was a young Englishman who enticed another young Englishman into a dismal swamp and for the sake of his money shot him in a brutal and cowardly way from behind. I met and knew afterwards several of the lawyers and people on the case and they all agreed that the murderer was a gentleman; in fact several of them said, "a thorough gentleman." Others said, "a perfect gentleman." Some of them had the idea that his victim was perhaps "not quite a gentleman" – but you'd hardly kill a man for that.

This shows, if any demonstration is needed, that a "gentleman" is not a *moral* term. As a matter of fact, all attempts to make it so break down hopelessly. People have often tried to sort out a class of people whom they call "nature's gentlemen." These are supposed to have it all – the honour, the candour (you can see it in their candid faces), all except the little touches of good manners and good English and the things that lie, or seem to lie, on the surface. They may be. But gentlemen don't mix with them.

Hence you can't qualify for being a gentleman by being good, or being honest, or being religious. A gentleman may be those things, but if he is, he never talks about them. In fact a gentleman never speaks of himself and never preaches. All good people do; and so they are not gentlemen. See how perplexing it gets? No wonder it worried us at school. For example can a clergyman be a gentleman? Certainly, if he keeps off religion. Or, for example, would a gentleman steal? He would and he wouldn't. If you left a handful of money right on a table near him, with no one in sight, no one to find out, he wouldn't steal it. Of course not; it's not the kind of thing a gentleman does. But if you left it in a bank account, he might have a go at it; but, of course, that's not exactly stealing; that's embezzlement. Gentlemen embezzle but don't steal.

And, of course, it goes without saying that being a gentleman isn't just a matter of wearing good clothes. You can't make yourself a gentleman by going to a good tailor. There is all the difference in the world between a man dressed like a gentleman and a tailor's dummy. No gentleman ever lets a tailor have his way with him. After the tailor has a suit measured to what he thinks an exact fit, a gentleman always has it let out six inches behind. You can tell him by that; and just when the tailor has the waistcoat what he calls "snug," the gentleman has it eased out across the stomach. You see, if you give a tailor his way he carries everything too far; his profession becomes a mania. All professions do. Give a barber his own way and he'll roll a man's hair into little ringlets, like a baby's coqueluche. That's why foreigners, as seen by a gentleman, are never well dressed and well shaved. They are too submissive to their tailor and their coiffeur. Hence instead of being well dressed and clean shaven, they are all overdressed and parboiled. This is what a gentleman means by a "French Johnny."

So one understands that a gentleman may dress as he likes.

I noticed an excellent example of this as related in a recent fascinating book of Australian travel. The scene was in that vast Australian empty country that you are not allowed to call desert. They speak of it as the "never-never country," or the "walla-boo" or the "willa-walla" – things like that. Out there – or in there – I don't know which you call it – there is nothing but sand and cactus and spinnifex, and black fellows, with occasional excellent shooting at great flocks of cockatoos, and an odd shot at a partridge or a pastoralist.

It was away off in this country that the travellers in the book I speak of came across a queer lost specimen of humanity, who had been living there twenty or thirty years – "a hairy, bushy-whiskered, unkempt individual. Grey hair grew on every part of his face. The only place where there was no hair was the part of the head where hair usually grows. That part was as bald as an egg. He had elastic-side boots but no socks. He had trousers but neither braces nor belt. The trousers were loose about the waist-band, and whilst he talked, when standing, he spent most of the time grabbing them and hitching them up just as they were on the point of falling down. It was constant competition between himself and the trousers – the trousers wanting to fall down and he wanting them to keep up."

But the odd thing is that when they came to talk to this man, there is no mistaking from their narrative that he was a gentleman. It was not only his contempt of a tailor that showed it. He had been to a public school, in the proper English sense as above. He still talked like a gentleman and, like a gentleman, had no word of complaint against a little thing like twenty years of sand.

When we say that this man "talked like a gentleman," how then does a gentleman talk? It is not so much a matter of how he talks but how he doesn't talk. No gentleman cares to talk about himself; no gentleman talks about money, or about his family, or about his illness, about the inside of his body or about his soul. Does a gentleman swear? Oh, certainly; but remember, no gentleman would ever swear at a servant – only at his own friends. In point of language a gentleman is not called upon to have any particular choice of words. But he must, absolutely must, have a trained avoidance of them. Any one who says "them there," and "which is yourn" and "them ain't his'n," is not a gentleman. There are no two ways about it; he may be "nature's gentleman"; but that's as far as you can get.

The more I look at this problem of the gentlemen the more I realize how difficult it is, and yet, in spite of everything, there seems to be something in it. One recalls the story of how Galileo was bullied and threatened by the Inquisition till he took back and denied his theory that the earth went round the sun. Yet as he came out from the tribunal he muttered to himself, "But it does really." So with the gentleman. There's something in it. This quiet man who never breaks his word and never eats with his knife; never complains of hard luck and wears his pants as he wants them; deferential to those below, independent to those above; the soul of honour, except in embezzlement; and when down and out goes away and looks for a wallaboo and enough sand and cactus to die in –

It's a fine thing. I'm sorry they failed at my school. I must have another go at it.

Literary Studies

The British Soldier

"Soldier, soldier, will you marry me,
With your knapsack, fife and drum?"

THE WAR brings the British soldier back into his own, as the nation's defender and the nation's hero. The only change is that in one sense everybody in Britain is now a soldier, and in another sense nobody is. The old "soldier" who spent his life in barracks, busy in war, boozy in peace, is now hard to find. In his place are a mass of "combatants," "mechanized units," "pilots," "bombers," "groundmen," "flying men," and "tank-mechanics." After the war they will be absorbed back again into the nation. It will turn out that the bomber was really a stock-broker, and that the submarine torpedo man was studying for the ministry – between shots. In other words the old-fashioned soldiers will have vanished, along with so many other old-fashioned things of England that we are told are to vanish after the war.

Poor old British soldier! He had only had about two and a half centuries of existence – since Charles the Second took over Oliver Cromwell's standing army. He was never welcome. The nation only accepted him on sufferance; drank his health in war time, and kicked him out of the pub in peace.

The little verse above, a fragment of a Victorian nursery

song, gives the measure of what a worthless fellow the nursery understood the soldier to be. Here he was, verse after verse, cadging and sponging on the poor girl, evidently a housemaid, lured to ruin by his red coat. First she sings to him:

> "Soldier, soldier, will you marry me,
> With your knapsack, fife and drum?"

And he sings back, miserable fellow:

> "Oh, no, my pretty maid, I can't marry now,
> For I haven't got a shirt to put on."

So the pretty housemaid gives the soldier a shirt and sings again for matrimony. But the soldier sings back for boots . . . and then for a hat, and so on endlessly. If there was an end, a final gift, it was not one for the nursery to hear.

After popular ballads had had their crack at the soldier, the comic poetry of the day took its turn in laughing at him. Here is Tom Hood, England's comic poet *par excellence*:

> Ben Battle was a soldier bold
> And used to war's alarms,
> But a cannon ball took off his legs,
> And he laid down his arms.

It appears that Ben Battle had "left his legs in Badajoz's breeches," an amusing memory of the fun of the Peninsula war. This may perhaps have been mere superficial laughter without malice. But there is a certain underlying meaning in it. An old soldier was taken for granted as a pauper, an object of charity. People may still recall the game, "Here comes an old soldier to town, pray what will we give him."

All that represents not what the British soldier was really like, but the character that the Victorian generations insisted on fastening on him. Kipling never wrote truer lines than the ones in which he speaks of the treatment of

Mr. Thomas Atkins at the hands of his fellow citizens:

> I went into a public-'ouse to get a pint o' beer,
> The publican 'e up an' sez, "We serve no red-coats here."
> For it's Tommy this, an' Tommy that, an' "Tommy 'ow's yer soul?"
> But it's "Thin red line of 'eroes" when the drums begin to roll . . .

The British public ever since early Victorian days and, indeed, for a century more or less before that, has always looked on soldiers of the ranks in that same way. In time of peace it resents their existence, deplores their low morals, and at first threat of war suddenly discovers that they are the "nation's defenders," the "boys in blue," or "in khaki," or the "thin red line of 'eroes" – made thin, no doubt, by low feeding in peace time. When the war ends they are welcomed home under arches of flowers, with all the girls leaping for their necks – and within six months they are expected to vanish into thin air, keep out of the public houses and give no trouble.

This attitude is all the more strange as contrasted with the typical British attitude towards the "sailor." Fact, fiction and fancy have enveloped the British sailor with qualities as endearing as those of Mr. Thomas Atkins are, supposedly, offensive and discreditable. The sailor is a "Jolly Jack Tar" – the more tar on him the better. It is his business to be perpetually drunk and "to take his Nancy on his knee" – the same Nancy who as a housemaid won't walk out with Mr. Atkins because she "doesn't hold with soldiers." But the Jack Tar stuff gets the girls every time. In return, they are supposed to take all his money, clean his pockets out and, when it's all gone, send him off to sea again. The Jolly Jack Tar is supposed to have "a wife in every port," but if Tommy Atkins in barracks ever ventures on having a Mary or two, there's a terrible fuss about it.

Think of all our ballads, poetry and songs that exalt the life of a sailor:

In No. 9, Old Richmond Square,
Mark well what I do say!
My Nancy Dawson, she lives there,
She is a maiden passing fair,
With bright blue eyes and golden hair,
But I'll go no more a-r-o-o-ving,
For you, fair maid.

Turn on the gramophone of recollection and over it comes a mingled melody of ballads in exaltation of the sailor and the sea: *"Stretch every stitch of canvas, boys, to catch the flowing wind."* – *"Sailing, sailing, over the bounding main, Full many a stormy wind shall blow ere Jack comes home again –"*

And as the sounds die lower and fainter one catches at last among them the requiem of the dead, the dirge for the sailors claimed by the sea:

Here's to the health of poor Tom Bowling,
The darling of the crew!
Nor more he'll hear the wind a-rolling
For death has broached him to!

How the deep sounds echo and reverberate like the boom of the sea itself.

And all of this – this national tribute of romance, of affection, of gratitude – how much has the soldier? Little, mighty little – at least in life. Our poets, apart from Kipling, always sing of his death, never of his life:

Half a league, half a league, half a league onward,
Theirs not to make reply, theirs not to reason why, theirs but to do or die . . .

Exactly. Theirs not to make any trouble! Neither in life, nor in death.

Students of literature will think to contradict me by reminding us of odd notes that sound in our poetry in praise of the soldier's life. Here's Shakespeare (he *always* is, right on the spot). Is it Iago singing? I forget.

Then clink to the cannikin, clink,
Why shouldn't a soldier drink?
For life's but a span, so enjoy it who can,
And clink to the cannikin, clink.

But better students of literature will tell us that this apparent exception proves the rule. Such drinking songs as these are meant to show what a wicked fellow the soldier is, how essentially without serious thought of a future life – in short, hell for *him*.

To understand this attitude we have to look back into history. The English, historically speaking, always hated "soldiers" – "paid men," as the word literally means, men hired to kill instead of fighting for anger's sake. An Englishman could look after himself; his house was his castle. There were no regular soldiers in England till Charles II, as said above, kept over some of Cromwell's standing army as a permanent force (the Coldstream Guards, etc.). William of Orange added to it. But, even with that, the power to keep an army was granted by Parliament so grudgingly that it went on only from year to year. The Supply Act only granted money, and the Mutiny Act only sanctioned discipline by legislation renewed every year. Without that, the army would come to a full stop for want of pay, and the officer's authority vanish for want of legal sanction. Without the renewal of the act, if an officer said, "Eyes right!" the soldier might answer, "Don't disturb me; I'm looking at something pretty good." This was true, in all peace time, up to the advent of the present war.

So the unhappy soldier had to pay for the sins of an evil profession. His treatment and his pay reflected this. So late as the early years of Queen Victoria's reign, the soldier lived in barracks without heat or ventilation; slept two, and even four, in a bed and was swept off by disease like vermin. There was little public heed of it. There were so many paupers and people of despair in the "merry England" of a century ago that recruits were always findable; the Queen's shilling could keep pace with Death.

The Victorian soldier's pay was twopence halfpenny a day, but there were so many odd charges and deductions at the start that a recruit might not get any pay at all for four months. The soldier lived under a savage code of flogging and punishment. He got no education. Before the Board schools of 1870 most soldiers could not read or write. The recruit was given (after 1829) a little record book (which he could not read) with a sample name in it, Thomas Atkins. That stood for him. Later he turned it to glory.

Thus a soldier was supposed to be a disreputable sort of person, whose aim in life was to get housemaids "into trouble." Soldiers, not *officers*! That was entirely different. Just as common soldiers had too little, so officers had too much in the long stretches of Victorian peace. These were the days before modern inventiveness had turned an officer's life into industry and algebra. An officer in between wars was supposed to do nothing – except to go to lawn parties, hunts, drags – God knows what; I forget the names of their entertainment – and accept the role of the pampered darling of the ladies. Every now and then there came along a "little war" and thither the officer went to play his part with infinite courage and no algebra; conquered the natives till they said "Quit!" then taught them how to play cricket.

How times have changed! One thinks now of European expansion, and the expansions imitated from it, as one vast horror of flaming gas and tearing detonations – how different from the days when Quanko Sambo, laying down his assegai, took up a cricket bat to develop his marvellous native ability at a cut to the off, and his permanent native inability to stand firm against a fast leg break. . . . Of the "little wars" of the time of which I speak, were the Abyssinian and the Ashanti, and the second Afghan and the first Boer – all of that enough and plenty, if all mixed with a period of service in India to give the officer his right to tea and muffins and the favour of the fair sex in the intervening intervals of leisure; enough to rank him above the curate, the doctor, the lawyer and the banker; as for the "business men" they were not yet respectable. The officers, all feathers and whiskers, ruled the roost.

But, oddly enough, the reasoning that created the social esteem of the officer was not applied to Mr. Thomas Atkins. He was in all the wars, big or little, just as much as his officer – but he got no thanks for it at home. I think one reason was that in the "Victorian" period of peace, from Waterloo to the Crimea, there was, literally, a generation who went into the army as young men after 1815 and served a whole lifetime, from subalterns to colonels, and never heard a shot fired except blank cartridges at a review. And here was a corresponding British public, the public of Charles Dickens's time, who had grown to forget war, who were absolutely removed from all possibility of invasion or civil war, who could not foresee in fancy the days of falling bombs – such a nation, sunk in the utter security of peace, sunk, by millions, in the utter hopelessness of poverty, what could they know or realize of soldiers? Soldiers! To the working men of the Chartist days, soldiers meant the men with guns called out to shoot down workmen in the massacre of Peterloo (1819). Soldiers, yah! just butchers with red coats. Honestly, ever so many workmen in England felt like that in the period of Victorian Peace. And officers! To the plain people, outside of society, great and small, officers, just fuss and feathers, India and hot curry. . . .

Turn over the pages of *Punch*, which began its life as a radical paper of protest and grew with years to the mellowness of saddened wisdom, and there you will see the officer and the soldier, in their Victorian feathers and in their Victorian "pubs."

No pages reflect this attitude more than the volumes of Charles Dickens, a repository of social history. Dickens had, with all his genius, the narrow short sight of his day and class, sentimental tears for poverty but no vision to remove it except by inviting everybody to be as noble a fellow as himself. War to Dickens was needless and silly;

foreigners, comic people, who lacked stability; officers, fops; soldier, loafers. Here and there, I admit, are bright exceptions (for I know my Dickens as a Scottish divine knows his Bible); I can recall of course Mr. Bagshot, and Trooper George. But speaking by and large, the whole military art was, to Dickens, either needless or comic. Witness the famous Chatham review in *Pickwick*, or the stock figure of the "recruiting sergeant," as in *Barnaby Rudge* and elsewhere – the Sergeant with the King's shilling – an engine of temptation and corruption to the young – seducing young men into "going for a soldier!"

It was only as the old standing army was passing away, at the close of the century, to give place to the new Nation under Arms, that the "soldier" began to come into his own. ... The South African War rediscovered Thomas Atkins as a "Soldier of the Queen," and sang invocations to him as a "good 'un heart and hand," as a "credit to his calling and to all his native land!" ... But before the change had time to be more than begun, the Great War of 1914 swept away the foolish complacency of Victorian Britain and set in a true light the values that had been disregarded.

But why, as the comedians say, why rake all that up now? So that we'll know better next time.

The Mathematics of the Lost Chord

EVERY ONE is familiar with the melodious yet melancholy song of "The Lost Chord." It tells us how, seated one day at the organ, weary, alone and sad, the player let his fingers roam idly over the keys, when suddenly, strangely, he "struck one chord which echoed like the sound of a Great Amen."

But he could never find it again. And ever since then there has gone up from myriad pianos the mournful laments for the Lost Chord. Ever since then, and this happened eighty years ago, wandering fingers search for the Lost Chord. No musician can ever find it.

But the trouble with musicians is that they are too dreamy, too unsystematic. Of course they could never find the Lost Chord by letting their fingers idly roam over the keys. What is needed is *method*, such as is used in mathematics every day. So where the musician fails let the mathematician try. He'll find it. It's only a matter of time.

The mathematician's method is perfectly simple – a matter of what he calls Permutations and Combinations – in other words, trying out all the Combinations till you get the right one.

He proposes to sound all the Combinations that there are, listen to them, and see which is the Great Amen. Of course a lot of the combinations are not chords at all. They would agonize a musician. But the mathematician won't notice any difference. In fact the only one he would recognize is Amen itself, because it's the one when you leave church.

He first calculates how many chords he can strike in a given time. Allowing time for striking the chord, listening to it and letting it die away, he estimates that he can strike one every 15 seconds, or 4 to a minute, 240 to an hour. Working 7 hours a day with Sundays off and a half day off on Saturday, and a short vacation (at a summer school in Mathematics), he reaches the encouraging conclusion that *if need be* – if he didn't find the Chord sooner – he could sound as many as half a million chords within a single year!

The next question is how many combinations there are to strike. The mournful piano player would have sat strumming away for ever and never have thought that out. But it's not hard to calculate. A piano has 52 white notes and 36 black. The player can make a combination by striking 10 at a time (with all his fingers and thumbs), or any less number down to 2 at a time. Moreover he can, if a trained player, strike any 10, adjacent or distant. Even if he has to strike notes at the extreme left and in the middle and at the extreme right all in the same combination, he does it by rapidly sweeping his left hand towards the right, or his right towards the left. There is a minute fraction between the initial strokes of certain notes, but not enough to prevent them sounding together as a combination.

This makes the calculation simplicity itself. It merely means calculating the total combinations of 88 things, taken 2 at a time, 3 at a time and so on up to 10 at a time.

The combinations, 2 notes at a time

Are $\frac{88 \text{x} 87}{1 \text{x} 2}$ 3,828

For 3 at a time $\frac{88 \text{x} 87 \text{x} 86}{1 \text{x} 2 \text{x} 3}$ 109,736

For 4 at a time $\frac{88 \text{x} 87 \text{x} 86 \text{x} 85}{1 \text{x} 2 \text{x} 3 \text{x} 4}$ 2,331,890

For 5 at a time	$\frac{88 \times 87 \times 86 \times 85 \times 84}{1 \times 2 \times 3 \times 4 \times 5}$	39,175,750
For 6 at a time	$\frac{88 \times 87 \times 86 \times 85 \times 84 \times 83}{1 \times 2 \times 3 \times 4 \times 5 \times 6}$	541,931,236
For 7 at a time	$\frac{88 \times 87 \times 86 \times 85 \times 84 \times 83 \times 82}{1 \times 2 \times 3 \times 4 \times 5 \times 6 \times 7}$	6,348,337,336
For 8 at a time	$\frac{88 \times 87 \times 86 \times 85 \times 84 \times 83 \times 82 \times 81}{1 \times 2 \times 3 \times 4 \times 5 \times 6 \times 7 \times 8}$	64,276,915,527
For 9 at a time	$\frac{88 \times 87 \times 86 \times 85 \times 84 \times 83 \times 82 \times 81 \times 80}{1 \times 2 \times 3 \times 4 \times 5 \times 6 \times 7 \times 8 \times 9}$	571,350,360,240
For 10 at a time	$\frac{88 \times 87 \times 86 \times 85 \times 84 \times 83 \times 82 \times 81 \times 80 \times 79}{1 \times 2 \times 3 \times 4 \times 5 \times 6 \times 7 \times 8 \times 9 \times 10}$	4,513,667,845,896
For all combinations		5,156,227,011,439

This gives us then an honest straightforward basis on which to start the search. The player setting out at his conscientious pace of half a million a year has the consoling feeling that he may find the Great Amen first shot, and at any rate he's certain to find it in 10,000,000 years.

It's a pity that the disconsolate players were so easily discouraged. The song was only written eighty years ago; they've hardly begun. Keep on, boys.

The Passing of the Kitchen

I HAVE A friend in my home town in front of whose modest house on the highway appeared a little while ago the sign "Tourists." Meeting him casually, I asked: "How are you getting on with the tourist trade? Are you getting any?" "Fine," he answered. "You see, it's all in the way you treat them. Tourists come to the house and we show them up to their bedroom and after a while the wife goes up and says: 'Now you come right on down to the kitchen. That's the place for you.' "

With which as my text, I will venture to assert that the kitchen is, and has been for generations and centuries, the most human part of any establishment.

Personally, like all my aging generation, from actual experience I know what a kitchen used to mean. In the Canadian country setting in which I was brought up sixty years ago, the kitchen was *par excellence* "the room" of the house. It was the only room with any size to it and the only room where it was always warm. A kitchen stove well filled with split hemlock maintained a heat of anything from 100 degrees Fahrenheit to about 1000 degrees Centigrade. You regulated the heat you wanted by the distance you sat from it. I am told that a kitchen of today can be regulated to an even 70 degrees by automatic stoking that is done in the cellar. On the other hand, we had the fun of moving our chairs backwards and forwards. These old kitchens when the farm-houses were laid out were practically the one room of the house. The others were just small spaces built off it. Later on, as the farmers got richer – or no, I don't quite mean that, as they got a little further into debt – they added a room called the "parlor." This was a swell room with an oilcloth on the floor and what was called an "organ" on which the girls of the family learned to play *Pull for the Shore, Sailor*. But the "parlor" proved a false start – it was too good for daily occupation; so after a while it was used only for funerals, and the kitchen came into its own again.

The typical Canadian "cooking stove" of those days was a broad, flat affair with six "lids" on its top and two divisions to it underneath, the firebox and the oven. It didn't have any of these gadgets and contrivances that turn the kitchen range of today into a marvellous piece of machinery. I have before me as I write a beautiful little booklet of a modern kitchen firm, containing pictures of all sorts of these contrivances of our up-to-date day.

Here, for example, is a wonderful little thermostatic dial which tells you the number of degrees of heat in the oven, without having to open it and put your face in as we used to. We couldn't have used that; if the kitchen stove was too hot there was nothing for it but to eat your dinner half an hour sooner. Cooking in those days was like navigation – a lot of chance to it. Here in the same booklet is a "ventilating fan above the stove to prevent cooking odors from reaching the rest of the house." The apparatus would have made no hit sixty years ago. The "cooking odors" were often the best part of the dinner.

After dinner, in the old days, came the "dish-washing" with a commotion on the scale of a charge of cavalry. The women worked at it with spirit; the dishes, like the cavalry, coming together with a glorious crash and with the casualties counted afterwards. Nowadays, in the pretty little kitchen I've been admiring in a picture, it's all different. Hot water runs at the turn of the tap. The dishes, as soon as they pass into the gleaming enamelled cabinet sink, seem instantly again things of beauty – just, as Burke said, "vice lost half its evil when it lost its grossness." A little "treatment" in the roomy looking basin and on to the drain boards, and the dishes will be clear back to virtue.

The kitchen, as I say, was the *real house* in our pioneer days. Indeed, if you have a taste for what is called archaeology, and go further back than that, you find that houses only came to be built as a shelter around the kitchen fire. Primitive men cooked their food at an open fire built on stones. But that meant that, if it was windy, the smoke would blow all over the place. So after, let us say, ten thousand years (their minds moved slowly) it occurred to some one to make a sort of wall of earth and stones on the windward side of the fire to keep the wind away. After this brilliant novelty had been popular for another ten thousand years, the device was found of building the wall around all four sides. From that to putting a roof over it was a mere step – not more than a thousand years! After that most primitive men "rested" and their houses – a wigwam, an igloo, or what-not – remained at that, a cooking fire walled in and fairly well covered over.

Now, if you don't believe this theory, that the kitchen was the house, you can go and see the proof actually in England, in the famous kitchen of the Abbot of Glastonbury. It still stands as a beautiful eight-sided stone house, with a roof tapering up to a peak where hung a lantern. It has size to it. When you undertake to feed a mediaeval abbot and a hundred monks and lay-brothers who have nothing to do all day but sing and eat, you have a real job. The Abbot's kitchen was about forty feet across each way. Even at that it was only one of a lot of celebrated kitchens of the Middle Ages. Several Abbeys, like those of Durham and Gloucester, had kitchens over thirty-six feet wide. But the triumph of all is found in the kitchen built by Cardinal Wolsey for the college that he founded, Christ Church, at Oxford, still the marvel of the tourist. Wolsey, like all great men, when he did a thing, did it on a big scale. Just as Cheops of Egypt needed a pyramid on his gravestone, and Cecil Rhodes about a hundred square miles on the Matoppo Hills, so

Wolsey, when he made a *kitchen*, saw to it that it *was* a kitchen. He had no use for underfed students. Learning, we are told, maketh a full man, and Wolsey's idea was to make the students full first so that they'd learn more easily. So the kitchen was made on such a proportion that you could roast an ox whole over one of its fires; and over another was a huge "turnspit" on which you could spike about a thousand birds at a time.

If you think these details were mere display, you only show that you don't understand the great part eating played in the Middle Ages. What else was there to do? No movies, no radio, no lectures on Cosmic Evolution – nothing but to fight and make love and eat. And as you kept running out of enemies and running out of girls, it left nothing but eating.

The size of the feasts was appalling. When King Edward IV (1467) wanted to express his delight at the consecration of Bishop Neville as Archbishop of York, he felt that a fitting religious touch would be given to it by a feast – all free for everybody. He invited 6,000 guests, and they all came. (They will every time!) The menu included roast mutton (1,000 sheep), a veal entree (304 calves), a side dish of 304 hogs, an "*entrements*" of 2,000 geese and 1,000 capons, along with a trifle of 13,500 birds. For anybody who wanted "another helping" there were 1,500 hot venison pastries, and 13,000 fancy tarts and jellies.

That sounds unbelievable, doesn't it? But it is all in an old Latin book called *Antiquitates Culinariae*. Of course, the feast went on for days and days, lasted till the guests began to leave because they had an engagement at another feast.

Now the odd thing was that when they cooked these vast banquets in the mediaeval kitchens, everything was done by hand labour in the simplest fashion. It never occurred to these people to look for mechanical contrivances, such as "mincers," "mixing machines," "cutters" and "parers" and the fancy cookers that replace human hands. The huge ox was hoisted up on a hook over the fire and a group of "turnspits" – unhappy little kitchen devils who lived and slept in the refuse – turned it round and round. The birds – the light stuff – were spiked together, a hundred or more at a crack, and turned on a spit in the same way. The furniture and appliances of the kitchen were of the same primitive simplicity. One or two enormous tables of oak planks hewed flat were placed to hold the huge copper cauldrons. Into these the head cook threw everything he could think of – nothing was measured, nothing was timed. Up went the cauldron over the fire, and when it was done – perhaps *he* knew what it was!

Compare with these our modern experts. I'd like to read this (I'm quoting again the latest *Kitchen Notes*) to Cardinal Wolsey or Archbishop Neville:

"In the kitchen of today, the work centres for preparation and storage, washing of food and utensils, and cooking and serving are arranged around the walls in proper sequence. The food comes in the back door and goes into the adjacent refrigerator and storage cabinets. Next in line comes the all-important sink complete with ventilated cupboards for the storage of vegetables and utensils, providing hot and cold tempered water to any part of the basin, a concealed spray fixture for rinsing on a rubber hose which pulls out from a niche and pops back when let go, and a removable cup-strainer in the outlet which catches crumbs and parings."

And yet I don't know whether that kind of thing would have made much impression on the Archbishop or the Cardinal. They had their own way in the Middle Ages. They didn't care much about mechanical exactitude. What they liked was the *personal* touch; and they had a grip on the cook which we have since lost. If anything went wrong with the banquet – well, there's no need to go into details – just say he never *cooked* again!

Yet, while he went strong, he was a person of great importance, even of rank or wealth. He had the privilege of walking into the hall in the procession, along with real gentlemen who had never worked in their lives and couldn't boil an egg.

The evolution of the kitchen seen from early times is odd enough. But odder still is the evolution of the cook. Take the cook of the Middle Ages with the long spoon and the turnspits and the cauldrons and what did he turn into, as mediaeval civilization faded away and the modern era replaced it? The cook of the great families, by the time of Queen Victoria and till yesterday, turned into a woman, usually a large, stout woman weighing from two hundred up, as shapely as a wet bologna sausage dressed in a black costume tied into divisions. She was called Mrs. Jennings, or Mrs. So-and-so, but nobody ever heard of her husband. Familiarly she was called "cook," and generations of English children got from her surreptitious tarts and delicacies meant for the grown-up people.

Then slowly "cook's" job began to be undermined. A woman called Mrs. Beaton conceived the daring design of feeding her own husband. Mr. Beaton died. Nothing, however, could be proved, and the matter was presently allowed to drop. Mrs. Beaton found no second husband and devoted her widowhood to making a list of all the things she had fed Mr. Beaton on. She published it under the name of *Cook Book*. Other rivals followed in her wake and cooking, which had been, like the church, a closed profession, was thrown wide open by the new "cook book."

The cook book, although nobody foresaw it at the time, did away with the cook. Anybody could be cook now. All you had to do was to follow the directions. "Take a pound of steak; beat it for an hour; then add ½ ounce of mace, ½ ounce of dice and beat it again for an hour; strain it, jump on it and add a gill of rosemary and anything else you haven't got . . . and then give it to them."

So, with the cook gone, and these simple directions to follow, and gadgets to do it with, the result has been that the kitchen, the real old kitchen, has gone too. There isn't any. Go out to dine in any of the new apartment households that Cupid opens every day, and the only cook that you find is the charming little hostess, who has just served the cocktails, dainty as if she never worked a minute in her life, and cool as a lobster salad. She just turns on a "control" to keep its eye on the roast, sets the soupometer for seventy degrees, turns on enough electric heat to freeze the cocktail, and there you are! Nothing to do but start the radio and wait for the guests and hope her husband gets shaved in time.

And when the little dinner is served, believe me, Cardinal Wolsey and his whole ox are just nowhere!

Come Back to School

FOR THE last several years this North American continent has been swept away by a wave of Adult Education. It is always being swept by waves – crime waves, drink waves, waves of religion, of speculation – till the back-wash of common sense dries it off again. But this wave of Adult Education, till the coming of the war slackened it, seemed flooding the whole country.

Adult education! I'm all for it. For some it means carrying on school all through life, never ceasing to learn; for others, beginning late what they had not the chance to begin early; making opportunity by overtime effort; supplying, by their own initiative and will, the defects imposed by adversity. That is adult education, and that is what it does for the community at large. I am, I say, all for it. If I could think of anything I didn't know, I'd take classes in it right now, at seventy-two.

Only I don't like the name – adult education. I wouldn't want any one to call me an "adult." That word never seems quite right; it always sounds like a halfwit. Don't they have homes for adults? No? Well, surely there are adults in some of the homes, and you can hang an adult, can't you? And, of course, "education" is a tainted word. It carries still its old false suggestion that it is something everybody had as a child, like measles, and doesn't need any longer. Say to any man, "Look here, don't you think you need a little education, the kind they give to adults?" and see how he reacts to it.

But the reality of adult education, which is what I want to write about, is one of the big things of the world today. What it means is that all the world is going back to school.

Now here is one of the reasons for it. People are no sooner out of school than they have a wistful longing to get back to it. Boys and girls take school as an accepted routine, understood by convention to be a sort of hardship, a violence to be done to youth. The teacher, if a man, is understood to be a pretty hard lot, and if a woman, a mean kind of cat. The child who says "I love teacher" is the odd one out, and will go to heaven early. At best they say, "She's not so bad," or "He's all right out of school." But school is no sooner over for the last day than they begin to weave round it a gossamer web of retrospect.

Each year that passes adds to their wistful illusion. They go back after three years, and there are the same old bricks (still there) and the same old desk with their names cut on it – look, see it! And when they hear, after four years, the sound of the same old bell, at the old hour (no change), they almost break down. As the years go still farther, and get really *on*, they find out that the teacher (dead) was a grand man, a scholar of the real old type. All the real type are dead. In fact, as with the Indian, the only good teacher is a dead teacher. As for the woman teacher, they discover later on that she wasn't a woman at all, just a girl – young and timid. How it must have distressed her – the rough horseplay, and the classroom cut-ups. Too bad!

It is the same, of course, with college, only on a much bigger scale, just as a three-ring circus eclipses a local Fall show. All through college the students are counting up the time to get out of it. The minute they enter, they call their class not by the year it comes in but by the year in which it hopes to go out. "Rah! Rah! Forty-five!" they shout. Just as if a baby was christened "Old Jones." They count each course; they number each credit; they "finish" trigonometry; after the second year they are no longer "liable" to history; after the third "not responsible" for Shakespeare; at the end of the fourth they are all signed off and paid off like a ship's crew from a long voyage. They shout "Rah! Rah! Forty-five!" But the sound weakens in their throat. Open the gates again! Isn't there any way to get us back?

So that is why, as they get on in life, people form all sorts of service clubs and luncheon clubs and go and hear speeches. They pretend, of course, that what they want is current information; that they want to get posted – but it isn't so. They want to get back to school, just as an old sailor wants to get back on a deck, and an old actor to get back on the boards. So there they sit, listening, back on their school benches, and the tougher the subject, the better they like it.

In my city, as in everybody else's, the luncheon clubs prefer a lecture on "Egypt Before Christ" to a talk on "England After Churchill." A week or two ago, I met a group of my acquaintances coming out in a flock from their weekly gathering. "What was it today?" I asked. "Great stuff!" one answered. "Professor Drydout was talking on Babylonian inscriptions. I couldn't get it all; in fact, I missed a lot of it, but it was great stuff." You see, there's a peculiar charm in "missing a lot of it." It takes you back to the class in geometry at high school.

So the clubs, though the members wouldn't admit it, are really a sort of school, a branch of "adult education." You can prove it by realizing how unwilling they are to permit a "humorous" lecture. In their hearts they'd really like something funny, instead of Babylon, just as they like a joke in school. But dignity won't allow it. Fun isn't education. If you want to give them a humorous lecture you must call it something else – pretend that it's on "The Later Tendencies of Democracy," and fill it with stories about Pat and Mike, and what Bill Nye said to Josh Billings.

Meantime the clubs go on expanding information like ripples on a pond, and "expanding" with it the capacity to listen, the desire to know, the sense of interest – in short, all those things which are the very soul of real education.

All power to the luncheon speeches. I only wish I could hear them. But like all old professors, I lost the power of listening years ago. I couldn't listen to Mohammed for more than four minutes.

One must remember that, after all, the continuance of education, the process of learning, or of trying to, brings its own reward. Human knowledge at large, in the huge philosophical sense, may indeed be more or less lost and bankrupt, but for the humble, single individual there is always a sense of achievement in learning something, even if it isn't so.

It was the custom, in the far back days that we now call Victorian, to insist that knowledge, in the sense of the contemplation of the universe, brought a sort of warm satisfaction. The stars sang together. A harmonious world fitted its parts like nickel-plated joints. Knowledge, so the poet said, unfolded to their eyes its ample page rich with the spoils of time. Study was even recommended to the Victorian working class, as a kind of sedative to put them to sleep.

Oh, what a world of profit and delight, sang one blithering poet, *is open to the studious artisan*. It may have been in 1840. At present, he wouldn't get much of a feed out of it, not in a universe of matter that has dissolved into atoms which are now merely "fields of force" – the whole physical world just a sort of disturbance, a universe "expanding" with terrific rapidity, not where you think it is, "out there," but in a "time-space continuum," which beats the studious artisan right to the balkline. In short, there's nothing left except a mathematical frame – inside of which a world agonizes, while what we called civilization fights for its life. No, my poor artisan, go and look at another peep-show. Ours is no good.

But while that is true of the general outlook, the humble individual satisfaction in learning something still holds good. If there is conceit and vanity in it, it is too pardonable to notice. If there is mingled with its excellence a little false assumption of superiority over one's fellows, the recording angel will easily blot it out with a tear.

At least the conceit of learning is better than the boast of ignorance that used to vaunt itself as an aid to success. I say "used to"; it was in the days before the great depression chastened the great conceit. "Look at me," once said in my hearing a big business man, a great big one. "I can't do fractions." I looked at him. He couldn't. But I felt that even a small decimal would have done him good.

But education, unless we carry it forward, dies out of itself. It is like a flood stream that runs away in the sand, like a garden choked under weeds, like a dim lumber room covered deep with dust. Such becomes education, even for the college graduate, if he never goes on with it. What's left? More wreckage. He has heard of an isosceles triangle and remembers that you mustn't produce the sides, or God knows what happens. He remembers that the third declension of Latin was a heller, and that Plato thought what Aristotle didn't think, and Aristotle didn't think what Plato thought. That's the grand old education that Oxford and Harvard used to sell, and it's all right too, on condition that you keep it in repair. Otherwise, don't try to "fall back on it." You'll hurt yourself behind.

Compare with such neglect the bright and eager conceit of the "graduate girls" of, say, forty, who are "following a course" on Persian literature this Spring, at one another's houses; they "took up" Dostoievsky last Winter, took him up and skinned him alive. And they're all right as a class too, the graduate girls of forty, far better than a class in school. Far too much has been said of the bright mind of youth and far too little of the ripened sympathy of the adult. It is the difference between light flashed from the surface of the water and the shadows that lie below. Not even youth can have everything as its part. Give adult life its share. Take, for example, all that goes with the appreciation of literature, of poetry. Children have not lived long enough yet, have not yet known, thank God, enough of sorrow and of disillusionment to draw the full meaning from the page in which the world has written and cross-written the record of our lot.

Children, bright children, exult in the clash of words and revel in sentiment of which the reality is as yet unknown. Look at them as they gather round the piano, little children of ten and twelve, to sing "In-the gloaming-oh-my darling" – dragging out the words in a whine of ecstasy. "Will-you-think of-one-who loved you-loved you-dearly-lo-o-ong ago!" That's all right, dears; now run along to bed. People who look back across the years to lost love have no song for it; it lies too deep.

Children at school may exult in the boy's standing on a burning deck, rhyming with wreck. They may climb in the shades of night with the "Excelsior" boy – "going up," Heaven knows where or why, except as a prevision of the elevator. But when one reads such lines as *and the stately ships go on to their haven under the hill; but O for the touch of a vanished hand and the sound of a voice that is still* – the echo of that is not for minds still in the opening of the pilgrimage of life. That is why, to my thinking, the class of adults – or no, I won't call them that; I mean grown-up people – is better than a group of children.

This only means that "school" from its very nature has a lot of limitations – much of it must be more or less mechanical, cannot call forth the spontaneous interest and the power of reflection that later learning does. It is hard to be terribly keen on the alphabet. The ancient Phoenicians may have been so when they made it; but children up against S-O-so, D-O-U-G-H-do, fail to get the same thrill. Nor can you reflect much on the multiplication table. You may try to sit and think how queer it is that 9 x 6 is 54, but you've got to be sure that it *is*, first. In other words, education that stops with school stops where it is beginning.

There are certain phases of adult education which give it, in a sense, a sterner aspect than when seen in the voluntary class taking the hide off an author, every Winter evening on Wednesday. I refer to the cases where people have to work overtime, study in the hours that are meant for recreation, as part of a determined drive against adversity. But even there it's not as bad as it seems. Some of our greatest minds have done their lifework in that way.

One case is that of John Stuart Mill. People think of Mill as the author of *Liberty and Political Economy*, and do not realize, or never knew, that Mill's "day's work" in life was not literature. All that was overtime. In the day, Mill worked in the London office of the East India Company, in the department of correspondence with Native States – making abstracts of the company's dealings with Ram Jam of Mysore and Dim Jim of Bengal. But by doing literary work he at last got free – to do literary work.

As a matter of fact, I may say with all modesty that I am myself another case. Fifty years ago I was a resident master in a boarding-school, a sort of all-day-and-all-night job, with a blind wall in front of it. To find a way out of it, and on, I took to getting up at five o'clock in the morning and studying political economy for three hours, every day, before school breakfast. This process so shapened my sense of humour that I earned enough money by it to go away and study political economy; and that, you see, kept up my sense of humour like those self-feeding machines.

But I didn't mean to speak personally.

Anyway, what's the good of talking about it? Come on. Let's get busy. Give me a book. I want to study something. I realize I don't know a darned thing. Hand me that multiplication table. I'll begin all over again.

What's in a Name?

Curiosities of Book Titles

THE TITLES of books that have come down from the past as part of the world's literature carry with them a sort of inevitability, as if they could not have been anything else; the *Canterbury Tales*, *Pilgrim's Progress*, *Alice in Wonderland*. This is especially so of the titles of the works of the Greeks and Romans. Their idea of a title was to name a thing exactly what it was. When Cicero proposed to write on friendship he called his little treatise *On Friendship*. When Livy wrote down the history of Rome he called his volume *The History of Rome* – not *Meet General Hannibal*. Indeed, for many, many centuries the aim of the writer in giving a title to his work was to indicate what it was about, not to make a sensation over its appearance. This was the prevailing fashion which led Dante to call his poem on Hell, simply *Hell* – as it was.

He couldn't think of anything more appropriate. Hence the earlier vagaries of titles only consisted in an anxious attempt to indicate not only what it was about, but all about it. Thus arose the elaborate explanatory titles that began to come into vogue in the seventeenth century. These were much stimulated in the writing of religious tracts and controversies, since, notoriously, a preacher finds it hard to stop. Compare – "*Meat out of the Larder, or Meditation concerning the necessity; End and Usefulness of Affliction with God's children*." Even the moderate and sagacious Adam Smith would have thought "*The Wealth of Nations*" far too snappy a title and called his immortal treatise an "*Inquiry into the nature and causes of the wealth of Nations.*" Malthus who followed Adam Smith with his *Essay on Population* which became and remained one of the world's books, presented it to the world with the title, "*An essay on the principle of Population as it affects the Future Improvement of Society, with remarks on the Speculations of Mr. Godwin, Mr. Condorcet and other writers.*"

It was perhaps in the realm of the drama that titles, at least in England, broke away from literalism to figurative and allusive forms. *Henry IV* is as plain a title as who should say *George VI*, but *As You Like It* is as up-to-date as next week. Unlike Shakespeare, Molière sticks to titles as self-evident as those of Caesar or Cicero – *Le Bourgeois Gentilhomme*, *Le Malade Imaginaire*, *Le Médecin Malgré Lui*. From Shakespeare on we have a string of such play-titles so familiar in their celebrity that their first peculiar novelty is forgotten, such as *Every Man in His Humor* or *She Stoops to Conquer*.

As the writing of fiction grew and stories multiplied, it was inevitable that a lot of them would run to the form of – *The Story of John Smith*, or the *Adventures of John Smith* – and hence simply *John Smith*, the familiar form of a proper name as a title: compare the long list that begins with *Humphrey Clinker*, *Roderick Random*, *Masterman Ready*, *Harry Lorrequer*, *David Copperfield*. When these have been sanctified by use and canonized by success we forget how purely neutral they are of themselves. At times the *sound* of the name carries aptness, either as a trifle comic (*Peregrine Pickle*) or as suited to the character, as *Charles O'Malley*, for a dashing Irish soldier. Many such titles have originally something in front of them, that got dropped from common citation, forgotten and very often not now inserted on the title pages of reprinted books, as with Fielding's two novels, *The History of Tom Jones, a Foundling*, and *History of the Adventures of Joseph Andrews and his friend Mr. Abraham Adams*. The book that we commonly call *Gulliver's Travels* had as its real title the legend, "*Travels into Several Remote Nations of the World by Lemuel Gulliver, first surgeon and then a captain of several ships*."

Very often, too, the neutral personal title of a book was pieced out with a sub-title, as with Fenimore Cooper's *Lionel Lincoln, the Leaguer of Boston*. But the use of sub-titles, or rather, second titles, is as fatal as the drink habit. They are apt to keep on and on till they get to comic forms, like: *James O'Hooligan, or the Irish Patriot, or Dagger and Dog in Donegal*. Its example is imaginary but the real ones are just as good.

It remained for Mr. Robert Benchley, whose humour is one of the bright spots of a stricken world, to catch the full value to the humourist of these alternative and unconnected titles. With the simple direct vision of genius he christened one of his books of sketches, "*David Copperfield, or Twenty Thousand Leagues Under the Sea*." The point is that there is no way for anything to be *both that* at once. The reader was lost between indignation and curiosity, bought the book and therewith forgot all about the title. A similar trick of the ingenuity of inventive genius is seen in Mr. Benchley's latest title – *After 1903 – What?* The reader is under the impression that we *know* what, and he can't see why Benchley doesn't. The humour of wilful imbecility lives forever.

If a gold medal were awarded for the most idiotic of titles, Victor Hugo would have received it, by acclamation, were it not that the advice of his horrified friends saved him from it. Hugo, living in exile in the Channel Islands, had just completed the striking story which he proposed to call, and later did call, by the fine title *The Toilers of the Sea* (*Les Travailleurs de la Mer*). All readers recall in it the desperate struggle under water of the fisherman seized by an octopus. But it so happened that Hugo's bottle of ink, a large one, with which he had begun the opening page of the story, ran out just as he wrote the concluding page. Nothing would do but he must re-name his book, "*A Bottle of Ink and Its*

Contents." Hugo, with the egotism of authorship, could not see the trivial vanity of such a title.

Almost on par with this idiocy are titles which are made out of some well-known phrase or familiar allusion, with which there is no real connection and which is merely dragged in because it is well known. Thus Frank Stockton, widely known as a novelist and humourist fifty years ago – used the title *A Bicycle in Cathay*. This was supposed to make a merry contrast with *A Cycle in Cathay*, a phrase taken out of Tennyson's poem (Locksley Hall) and often quoted in those days: "better fifty years in Europe than a cycle in Cathay." But the story was not laid in China and the application is so forced as to be painful. Take any well-known phrase, or short quotation, and you may be sure that somebody has already used it, or that somebody presently will. We either have already, or will have soon, novels called *To Be or Not to Be*, *What's in a Name*, *Coming Through the Rye*, and so on endlessly.

But turning back a minute to the use of reinforced titles, with sub-titles and appendages, we may note that perhaps the most colossal example of this sort of thing is found in the original title of Dickens's *Martin Chuzzlewit*. The book is now, or was even in Dickens's lifetime, printed with just the name as a title. But when first written, in instalments, the title read, *The life and adventures of Martin Chuzzlewig* (not yet *Chuzzlewit*), *his family, friends and enemies, comprising all his will and his ways with a historical record of what he did and what he didn't, the whole forming a complete key to the house of Chuzzlewig*."

Talking of Dickens, it may be recalled that no one gave more thought to titles and names, or attached more importance to them. He himself would have strenuously denied – he was fond of strenuous denials – that David Copperfield was a neutral name; he would have drawn our attention to the various trial and error titles that the book carried at its inception. He would have shown us that both David Copperfield himself and the story which embodied his life were first very differently christened: "*Mag's Diversion, being the personal history of Mr. Thomas Mag the Younger of Blunderstone Hall.*"

Indeed Dickens – an artist in the phonetic significance of names – felt that sounds and syllables carried undercurrents of meaning. Vocal tones, the philologist tells us, antedate speech; names and sounds have queer buried values like the growls of dogs, the satisfied grunts of feeding hogs and the murmur of the turtle dove – *lenis susurrus sub nocte*. Thus when Dickens saw the word *Pickwick* on a coachmaker's sign, he felt it was just the name for the kind of man he had begun to think of. When he wanted a name for a young man round whose fate are to gather dark clouds of mystery and murder, he called him *Edwin Drood*. But he did not name him so until he had tried out and rejected an assorted list of names, fitted into a list of suggested titles.

TITLES

Edwin Drood
The Loss of James Wakefield
James' Disappearance
Flight and Pursuit
Sworn to Avenge It
One Object in Life
The Kinsman's Devotion
The Two Kinsmen
The Love of Edwin Brood
The Loss of Edwin Brude
The Mystery in the Drood Family
The Loss of Edwin Drood
The Flight of Edwin Drood
Edwin Drood in Hiding
The Loss of Edwin Drude
The Disappearance of Edwin Drude
The Mystery of Edwin Drude

As a matter of fact Dickens presently adopted the rather mechanical method of writing out for himself a list (there are 230 names in it) of *Available Names* from the Privy

Council Education Lists – drawn up and headed *Girls*, then *Boys*, *more Boys*, and *more Girls*. Thus does genius itself fall back on artifice; but not, be it noted, till genius has first shown where artifice may operate. Some of the names are quite unbelievable, such as *William Why* and *Sally Gimblet* and *Sophia Doomsday*. Among the actual surnames is *Sapsea* which was used in *Edwin Drood* and which no doubt many readers dismissed as impossible.

We spoke above of historical titles and how Mr. Woodward in his admirable biography invites us to *Meet General Grant*. No doubt if he had called it *The History of Ulysses S. Grant* we might have missed meeting him. Indeed it seems to be the case that readers nowadays won't take their history "straight." The *History of England* is all right, but Mr. André Maurois put a new slant to it and turned it into a best seller by calling it *The Miracle of England*. *The Decline and Fall of the Roman Empire* did well enough for Gibbon. But a new history of the Byzantine Empire recently appeared as *Emperors, Angels and Eunuchs*. It sounds more exciting.

Naturally enough in the vast market for popular storybooks today there is a tremendous pressure put on writers to try to find titles which attract at sight – "Mysteries" so mysterious that the very name of them ties us in a knot, "Horrors" so horrible that they can reach us through a bookstore window. In Wilkie Collins's day such a title as *The Woman in White* sent a chill down the Victorian spine: today we have to ring the changes on *The Murder on the Links*, *The Murder on the Express*, *The Murder in the Sky* – if there's any new place to "lay" a murder, let's have it and get it over.

Such is the craze for novelty in titles that nowadays when the reviewers of the magazines review a book they won't even write it up over its own title – they make up a new one. If the author calls his book *Six Months in Mexico*, the reviewer heads up his talk on it as *Down Under the Rio Grande*. *Across Czechoslovakia* reappears as *Checking Up on the Checks*. This is especially so when the reviewer and his magazine do not find enough "pep" in the original title. *Notes on Insect Life* has to become *Revelations of a Bug Man*.

Some time since I amused myself by reconstructing what would have been the effect if this method had been applied to some of the great masterpieces of the past. The results, as far as I recall them, converted Caesar's *Bellum Britannicum* into *An Old Campaigner's Log: new volume of Memoirs on Savage Life in the British Isles*, and changed Milton's *Paradise Lost* into *Raising Hell, or Pen Pictures of Battles in the Sky*.

But of course the reviewers too, like the authors, must keep up to date and novel or get trampled under.

Who Canonizes the Classics?

ACCORDING to the practice of our oldest church, it takes about four hundred years to make a saint. That is to say, during that period one can't be just sure whether he's a saint or not. But if at the end of four hundred years his apparent saintliness has withstood the wear and tear of time, then a saint he is, indubitably and forever. Many of us no doubt received a pleasant shock of surprise, a year or two ago, when the venerable victim of Henry VIII, beheaded in 1535 and known in our school-books as Sir Thomas More, became henceforth Saint Thomas. I say a *pleasant* surprise – as helping to emphasize the continuity and permanence of society, a thing grievously in the doubt just now.

If therefore in the Spiritual Kingdom there are saints that last, there must be in the Republic of Letters authors whose work remains. But in this case we have no definite process of canonization. In a general way, the world at large refers to certain authors as "classic"; but how they got to be so, and who makes them so, becomes more mysterious the more you look at it.

As everybody knows, the word "classic" used to be used to indicate merely the literature of Greece and Rome. It was held commonly to include *all* the Greek and Roman books that had survived – no very great amount in any case, as a quite small library would hold the lot. But the Romans themselves had used the word a little differently. They meant by "classics" the *best* of their books. The word was the adjective from *classis* – an assembly, a fleet, a class. Oddly enough, when some one introduced for us the cheap word "classy" he reproduced exactly the old Latin *classicus*.

But the meaning of the word "classic" and of "the classics" has, within a generation or two, been altered, or rather expanded, to mean not only the ancient books, but also all such books of our own time as deserve from their excellence a prominent and permanent place in our literature. Thus Macaulay's works, no one doubts it, are "classics"; so too those of Emerson and of Hawthorne. So are not, if one may say it with all gentleness, those of the late Edgar Wallace. On the other hand every one thought, forty years ago, that George Meredith's books would prove to be "classics": and they haven't.

What, then, makes classics? Who decides what is on the list and what not? Are classics being written now, or will there be no more of them? Does the list indicate the books that are read, or the books that ought to be read, or the books that keep on being read? Must classics be serious, or have heaviness and lightness nothing to do with it? Do the *Bab-Ballads* get in along with the *Rubaiyat*, and Tom Hood sit beside Robert Browning? Does the mere fact that a vast number of people read and enjoy a book make it at once a classic?

Now I do not think that any one of these distinctions indicates the test as to what is or what is not a classic. The most widely read book in all the history of the world (as referring to one year's reading) was published in the last decade. Where will it be in five years? Mark Twain's *Innocents Abroad* is a classic and yet is as light as innocence itself. Karl Marx's *Capital*, another classic, is as heavy as gold. *Maria Chapdelaine* is a classic and was written yesterday. Chaucer's *Tales*, on the shelf alongside of it, are older than printing.

Many people are apt to presume that the classics have their place given to them by scholars and professors, that they are canonized over the heads of the plain people by the academic class. Those who think this feel a certain resentment. It is part of the general objection to what is called high-brow – a sort of assumed superiority which sweeps the area of art, music, and literature and takes away from the plain man the pleasure of his plain enjoyment. He stands condemned because he likes to hear his daughter at the piano play *In the Gloaming*, or to read aloud Ella Wheeler Wilcox's *Rock Me to Sleep, Mother*. Meantime the professor who condemns him reads Browning's *Sordello*, and goes into ecstasies over it.

The basis of this resentment of what is high-brow is no doubt sound; subconsciously, people know that a vast mass of aesthetic superiority is false, a substitution of affectation for reality. Very few people can stand the strain of being educated without getting superior over it. Every one must have noticed how professors of literature annex Shakespeare, and professors of history take over Napoleon, and leave the rest of us out. What we think doesn't matter.

But in the present case I don't think for a moment that professors make the classics. Indeed it is the other way round. In the field of letters, as apart from medicine and science, professors do not lead but follow. Their wisdom is always that of a post mortem. They made political economy after the industrial revolution, not before it. They explained democracy *after* the people created it, and it is not till the people have read a book for a hundred years that the professors can explain why. In other words the cart doesn't go before the horse. Not at all. The horse, the mass of human intelligence, draws along the cart of history in which stands the professor, looking backward and explaining the scenery. This is not said unkindly. If he looked forward he wouldn't see any more than the horse does; and the horse sees nothing.

Not the professors, then, nor yet the favour of courts and clergy, of kings and noblemen, can make a classic apart from merit. Louis XIV's *Académïe* only recognized what was there already. "You may admit Molière," wrote the

King. But Molière didn't need it. There is no royal road to learning, nor to authorship. One recalls Queen Victoria presenting to Charles Dickens with pathetic modesty her little book *Leaves from a Life in the Highlands*, and receiving in return Dickens's entire works.

Consider, if you like, how some of the classics came to take rank as such. Take Shakespeare. Here was an unknown person who had a wonderful trick of putting old stories together, so as to turn them into plays. There were lots of people doing it, or trying to. It was the chief creative art of the day: playgoing, playwriting, strolling players, mummers. It was the chief answer, among a nation who couldn't read, to the age-long demand of humanity – "tell me a story."

And Shakespeare could not only put a play together but he had an extraordinary gift of language. When a thing is well said, all ears listen to it. When Shakespeare's actor said, "tomorrow and tomorrow and tomorrow, creeps in this petty pace from day to day, . . . and all our yesterdays have lighted fools the way to dusty death" – even the people in the cheap seats, the groundlings, must have said "God save us!" And the thing went on and on. No board of judges, no favor of a court made Shakespeare Shakespeare. As far as I know, no professor ever sat on him till the Germans, the Schlegels, got at him, nearly two hundred years later.

Or take Walter Scott. There came a day when the people in Edinburgh walked up and down the street with their eyes glued to a book called *Waverly*, and looked up to ask perfect strangers, "Have ye read it?" Professors don't do that. And about twenty years after that all England was roaring over *Pickwick* – except the professors, who haven't started yet. They will, though. In about fifty years more they'll discover Dickens, as the church discovered Thomas More.

No, no – the classics are made so by the appreciation of the people at large. You can fool some of the people all of the time, and all the people, etc. – we remember what

Abraham Lincoln said. Yet not even appreciation will always do it. At times appreciation springs up as fast and withers as quickly as the seed in the bad ground. All the polite world once read Aphra Behn, thrilled over Ossian and shuddered at Mrs. Crowe. In our own time one has seen George Meredith pass to oblivion, and one sees every day the "Best Sellers" spreading as wide as sunshine, and passing as quickly as the day itself.

And what is more, even appreciation with the lapse of years may shift from its true basis to a false. Shakespeare is admired now, by the high-brows, for things he never thought of, for effects he never planned. Scholars dissect Chaucer and sew him up again all full of "purpose." The college taxidermists have whole museums full of stuffed authors. In the end it doesn't matter. Native appreciation lives on after the stuffing has fallen out.

The matter stands like this. There is a certain class and kind of literature that has the quality of universality. It has something in it that reaches the high and the low, the wise and the foolish, the educated and the illiterate. This quality in it makes it ring as true as a bell. After all, in this transitory life, we are all, high and low, educated and illiterate, on one and the same pilgrimage. The essential frame of this life is the same for all. The Anglo-Saxon who spoke of life as a bird passing a moment through a lighted hall and out into the darkness spoke down the ages to twenty generations. When Shakespeare said, "tomorrow and tomorrow and tomorrow," the words were as good yesterday as today.

What we call the classics are the books that have enough of this universal appeal to give them their place and keep them there. One might wonder why it often comes about that books seem written for but one class, or in a language largely out of common understanding, yet reach and hold a wide enough world to make them classics. The reason is, I think that appreciation is a queer thing running in sympathetic channels. Children listen, enthralled with things they cannot understand. Clergymen love sea-stories and sea-captains read theology. When a man sits buried in a book, it is not the man that you see and know that is reading. Deep down in him are antecedent generations – soldiers, pirates, martyrs, fading back to cave men. As he reads, the "universal" book is calling to one of them.

I remember, years ago, how an old gentleman of my acquaintance, the father of one of my classmates at college, but himself a plain business man, picked up one evening his son's copy of Kant's *Critique of Pure Reason*. He sat down and read it with absorption. "Fine," he said. He sat up late that night reading it; didn't finish it, so he told us next day, till nearly one o'clock. Always afterwards he said it was a great book. It must have hit him somewhere. Perhaps he was a far down descendent of the sculptor Rodin's *Thinker* – who could think without words.

And now I will say one further thing about the classics. *There are not going to be any more.* We have them all now, all that there are ever going to be.

I cannot imagine any judgement more likely to meet with instant dissent, and to be dismissed with contempt or laughter. It sounds like the opinion of an aging man, for whom the world is running out with his own years. Such judgements are familiar. But I do not think that this is one. As I see it, the pre-eminence of written books reached its height in the nineteenth century, when for the first time all the world went to school, and before all the world went to moving pictures and listened in on the radio.

In the nineteenth century it was still possible in a world as yet under-developed and under-explored, to reach with a new book a mark so far beyond the previous record that the book became a heritage. There is no such opportunity now. No one can be in political economy an Adam Smith or in political philosophy a John Stuart Mill, in fiction a Walter Scott or a Charles Dickens. The world of letters moves forward on a broad front, millions and millions all talking and reading, together. Each little increment of new excellence carries some one a moment into sudden notoriety – greater than that of the Mills and the Darwins – but a notoriety "gone with the wind" – vanishing as soon as achieved. We live in an age where universal competence is replacing individual eminence: or rather, since "eminent" is a comparative word, an age in which the eminent man only "sticks out" a little. I know a little boy who told me the other day that he could easily have won a race at his school except that there was another boy who could run faster. Of such stuff is present eminence made. One recalls Dickens's America, in which every other man was "the most remarkable man in the country." So it is in the Republic of Letters.

Not that you or I and the rest after us will ever realize that the classics have gone, that the list is closed, the booking office shut. Best sellers will still sweep over the landscape, remarkable books will convulse society, new works of philosophy will revolutionize human thought. But no one will live long enough to know that they didn't last, and that behind them in receding landscape of history Chaucer will be still telling tales – not better, but prior to other people's – and John Stuart Mill remain part of the world's history having had the good luck to live a century before Professor Jones.

So my prophecy of a classicless age to come is a safe one. By the time it's due, it won't matter. "You said at the last election," complained once an old farmer to me, "that the price of marsh hay would go up." "Yes," I answered, "but the election's over." So let it be with the withering grass of literature.

Among the Antiques

An Adventure at Afternoon Tea

A MAID OPENED opened the door. But Mrs. DeCarteret came flying down from upstairs in that impulsive way she has. "Now that's so nice of you to come," she said. "Let me take your coat and hat. Never mind, Milly. . . . You see I don't put them on the hat rack; we have pegs for them over here. But you *must* look at the hat rack before you go up. Isn't it just a darling?"

"I suppose," I began.

"Yes," she answered, "it's one of the things we got in Italy. It's a genuine Amalfi; you can tell it by the worm-eaten wood; of course it would fall to pieces at a touch. They guaranteed it would. But do come along upstairs to the den. I'm so glad to have got you here at last; you've been so naughty about coming. . . . But, if you don't mind, just lift your feet a little higher as you step over the rug."

"Is that –" I asked.

"Yes," said Mrs. DeCarteret, "it's a Louis Treize. How did you know? But then of course you know antiques. It's too old of course to step on. We picked it up, just ran into it by chance in France, at Ouen, in the Dordogne, just this side of Quon. Do you know Ouen?"

"As far as I –" I began.

"Oh, you ought to go there," said Mrs. DeCarteret. "Now do come up and we'll have tea. James will be home in a minute, because he knows you're coming. But (before we go up) do just look at this clock on the landing."

"Is that –" I asked.

"No, that's Dutch. It's an Artemus Yoops. Do you know his work at all?"

"I don't believe –" I began.

"James and I think that there is nothing like a Yoops. So of course when in Holland we kept looking all the time for a genuine Yoops, and at last we ran into this one – in the quaintest little shop, in Obersloopendam. Do you know Obersloopendam, at all?"

"No," I said, "I've never . . ."

"But you really *should* go there. Now this clock you can see – I mean a connoisseur can see – is an Artemus Yoops, because you can see his name scratched on the case. The A is quite plain, isn't it? It has only one hand; that's another mark of its being genuine. I get so amused sometimes when people, people who don't know, ask if it keeps good time! Of course its works were removed long ago; that was one reason for the high price. But now come along into our den! James and I call it our treasure house."

The "den" of the DeCarterets is a room spacious enough for Daniel and all his lions. All round it and in it and through it are "treasures" – on four legs, three legs, or two legs, or leaning or resting. None are for use. On the mantel are two Grecian ash trays, Phrygian, not for ashes. There is a Sèvres China tea set, not for tea, chairs not to sit on, and glasses not to drink from.

Mrs. DeCarterer sat down beside the tea things, the real ones, and asked, "One lump or two?" and I said, "Two," and she said she was so glad to have me there because she did so enjoy clever conversation.

I said, "Don't you think –"

But Mrs. DeCarteret was already talking about the Sèvres tea-pot; and after that about the little statuettes from Athens; and after that about the spinning wheel from Brittany; and after that she was just beginning about the Botticelli miniature from Italy, when DeCarteret came in.

"Ah, here's James," she said. "James can tell you all about these. We got them in Italy. We got such lovely things in Italy. Of course there is really nowhere like Italy. We got that in Milano. Do you know Milano?"

"No," I said, "I've never –"

"Oh, you really ought to go there. That particular miniature was one of the things that had belonged to the Splozza Family. They're one of the old Italian families, of the old nobility of the Church. We met Prince Splozza the present one. Do you know him?"

"No," I said, "I don't think I ever –"

"Oh, you ought to meet him – such a charming man. He has such a wonderful Palazzo in Milano, right near the Duomo – wasn't it, James?"

"Yes, just between the Duomo and the Corso, in fact right on the Via del Sploggio itself . . ."

"Such a dilapidated old place," interjected Mrs. DeCarteret, "and yet so perfect."

"Of course," DeCarteret went on, "they're all terribly hard up in a way, the Italian nobility. When we met Prince Splozza, he was wearing just a plain gun-metal watch – showed it quite openly – said it was all he could afford – said it quite simply, just like that. So I thought it over," continued DeCarteret, "and I sent away to Paris and got the most beautiful gold watch that could be bought. I was terribly afraid, of course, of hurting Prince Splozza's feelings."

"Did he take it?" I asked.

"At first not; he hesitated quite a time; insisted that I must take it away; he said he had no chain fit to wear with it."

"And so –"

"So I didn't say a word. I took it away and came back next day with the watch and a gold chain."

"And the Prince took it?"

"He did. He said that now he couldn't refuse – such *considerazione*, he said; that's the word he used. Italian is such a beautiful language, isn't it? You can hardly say it in English. No, the Prince said he could have wished he had a proper jewel box to lock up the watch and chain at night, but that he must take a chance on that."

"And so you –"

"So we got a lovely jewel box and this time we took no chance on a refusal, just shoved the box into the pocket of the Prince's dinner jacket when we dined with him at the Restoranto del Re – that is, he was dining with us, but he showed us where it was."

"And he was so charming afterwards," Mrs. DeCarteret broke in. "He introduced us to quite a lot of the nobility, particularly to his cousin, dear old Cardinal Paulzi; have you met him?"

"I am afraid –" I began.

"Oh, you really ought to – just the dearest old man, so frail, but as I said to James, he seemed to me the very picture of apostolic sweetness – so unworldly, like a child. He showed us his rings, and he admitted, dear old man, that they are his one worldliness. 'If I only had a diamond,' he said, 'but I suppose I never shall.' So what do you think we did? We went right away and that very same day brought back the most beautiful diamond!"

"And did he take it?"

"Take it? Why, of course, he was just like a child over it, just overjoyed! 'Oh!' he kept saying. 'How beautiful – and if I only had an emerald to go with it.' "

"So you –"

"So we got him an emerald ring. I wish you could have seen him, the poor old man – he quite broke down. Great tears rolled down his face. He could hardly speak. He just whispered when we were leaving him, 'If I only had a sapphire . . .' "

"Did you give him one?"

"Later, we sent one to him, when we could get one. They're not easy to find. So we sent it later on to him, sent it by Count Chiaro Chianti, a most delightful man, so soldierly, in fact an *aide-de-camp* to the King . . ."

"No, dear," interrupted DeCarteret, "that wasn't Count Chianti; that was Count Fosco di Bosco. . . ."

"No, James," said Mrs. DeCarteret. "I mean the one we gave the fur coat to."

"That wasn't the fur coat," said DeCarteret. "We gave Chiaro Chianti a rifle – or was he the one in the navy that we gave the rubber boots to?"

"I'm afraid I get them mixed," said Mrs. DeCarteret with a resigned sigh, "but they were really so charming, the Italians, I mean those of the old class with the high traditions. Such a pity we have so few people like them. . . . What, are you getting up, to go? I'm so sorry. It's so rare that one can enjoy worth-while conversation. Won't you have some more tea?"

"No thank you!" I said.

Then Mrs. DeCarteret remembered something. "Oh, James," she said, "I'm so sorry. I forgot to offer you any tea. Won't you have a cup?"

"No thanks," said DeCarteret, "really not. I'm going to have a scotch and soda in a minute."

He meant, when I was gone. It was hard to bear. But the Italian nobility have nothing on me.

"Good-bye," I said.

Sporting Section

What Is a Sport?

JUST WHAT is a "sport"? There's a thing I've wondered about more or less all my life. What do we mean by a "sport"? Mind, I'm not saying a "sportsman." Everybody knows what he is. A sportsman is a man who, every now and then, simply has to get out and kill something. Not that he's cruel. He wouldn't hurt a fly. It's not big enough. But he has that instinct from away back in the centuries that he's got to get out on the water or in the bush and kill something; or rather, not so much that he wants to kill it, as to crawl round after it, crawl under brush and stoop under boughs – noiseless, alert – pretending that he's a "bushman" of ten thousand years ago and that he wants to kill this thing and eat it. He *won't* eat it really; he'll give it to the chauffeur or the man at the gasoline station. As a matter of fact he doesn't need to kill anything at all, only just to put on an old pair of pants and pretend that there's something in the bush, even when in his heart he knows there isn't. In my part of the country – Simcoe County, Ontario – all the "keen sportsmen" (that's the word, "*keen*") go out after partridges every autumn though there hasn't been a partridge seen for nearly twenty years. You don't really need them for partridge shooting, just old pants, half a dozen cartridges and a hip flask. A sportsman who's a real sport will be quite satisfied with that.

Ah! there it is – a real "sport." Because it doesn't follow that every sport is a sportsman. For instance, a fisherman who comes home and tells the truth about the size of the fish that the other fellows lost is no sport. I don't mean that a sport is a liar; but there are times when you can't get the truth out of him.

So you see that there is no use trying to understand what a sport is by defining a sportsman. Nor does the dictionary help. The one I have beside me says "Sport (biol.)" . . . that means I imagine a "biological term" . . . "an individual variant from a general class, see also under *freak*, *nut*, etc." In other words, in that sense, scientifically a *sport* means such a thing as one of the citrons that sometimes grow on a melon plant, a single black raspberry among red and so on. In this sense the son of a Presbyterian minister who turns out a drunkard is a "sport," and another "sport" is the son of a lawyer who becomes a missionary. But none of that helps us very much.

The dictionary goes on to talk of "*sport* (etym.)." That means – I looked "etym." up in a dictionary, "etymologically," or "by derivation." And in this sense sport means, "a departure, a relaxation, a getting outside of oneself, see also under 'ecstasy,' 'idiocy' and 'mental alienation.' " That doesn't help either, does it? I don't think a sport is an idiot. He might be, I admit, and as a matter of fact lots of half-witted fellers are darned good sports. Several of the friends I like to go fishing with are only about half-witted, and some even more.

So you see, when the dictionary says that a sport is a freak or an idiot, it's all off the track. Neither will the recollection of individual cases help you much as to what a sport is. They all get mixed up with special circumstances. I remember that when I was a boy at school I thought a "sport" had to mean a man who kept a saloon, or at least never came out of one, weighed two hundred pounds, had a face like an angry sunset and wore a big diamond where his chin should have been. This notion of a sport as connected with loud neck-ties, pants with a check pattern as big as a Mercator's map, led many of us astray in those days. To be a "*sport*" seemed to mean taking a huge interest in prize fights, discussing when any one would lower the record of Maud S., and J.I.C. – no, no, they weren't women, but they were the fastest things, outside of women, that had turned up in the eighties. Let me see, Maud S. "did it in 2:40." You ask, "Did what in 2:40?" What? I don't know. I never knew. I was only a little boy at the time and it may have been kilowatt hours or miles to the gallon. Anyway it's what she did it in. And it always made me feel that if a sport had to sniff around stables all day, and talk mysteriously of whether the cops would break up the cock-fight next Friday, and which nigger beat who – then I didn't want to be a sport. Yet those of us who thought that way felt that that couldn't be the whole of it. Surely a sport didn't have to be full all the time to qualify.

There's another point occurs to me in this connection: *Must* a sport drink? I admit it's a pretty nice question. I will try to illustrate it from actual fact. I remember a case in point, years and years ago, of three "fellers" who went out to spend their vacation camping round Lake Simcoe, with a tent and a canoe. They dragged along with them a big jar of whisky; Lord knows they didn't need it; the fresh air was enough. They were just of the age between boys and men, at the time when a feller likes to stretch his limbs and say "makes a man feel pretty good, eh? this fresh air." But being "sports" they felt that open-air life would be incomplete without the jar of whisky. "What about a little snort, eh?" one of them would say, and the others, being challenged, had to say, "Right you are." Though as a matter of fact they were half sick with it already. In the morning, as they crawled red-eyed and bleary out of their little tent, one would say, "How about a little snifter?" and they had to begin again. Being sports, and out in the open where sports belong, they had to have "snorts" and "snifters" and "jolts," all day. Any one of them could have refused but he'd have been a pretty poor sport, if he had, wouldn't he? How glad those fellers were to get back to work in the city when the vacation was over, and have oatmeal porridge and coffee for breakfast with no one to say, "What about a little stick in it?" They certainly were glad. I know it, because I was one of them.

So you don't get much light there on a sport, or at least only a kind of will-o'-the-wisp effect to connect a sport with open air, and a sort of comradeship that won't say no.

You would think that you would get a truer idea of what a sport is if you consider the way in which we use the word in regard to games. But I am not so sure that you do. You get either too much light or too little. Our games are either "out to win" to the verge of ferocity, or willing to lose to the verge of vacuity. In cricket, for instance, you have a case in point. Here I speak of what I know. I played cricket, at least I had a cricket bat and played something, for years and years. As a matter of fact I once played in a big match at Ottawa, on the Government House grounds and made what they told me was a record for the ground – going in first in the first innings and being bowled out by the first ball, and going in last in the second innings and being bowled out by the first ball, that is, the last ball. The full technic of this is explained in an article below but cricketeers will understand it anyway.

So I may properly say that I speak as an expert when I talk of cricket. And there the code of "sport" is high; if the umpire says "out" you're "out"; you mustn't even hit him with your bat. If you're made to play square leg and get hit in the stomach with the ball because you were thinking of something else, you're supposed to say, when you can speak, "Sorry, old man!" – not sorry for yourself, but sorry for the bowler. You have to take it in the stomach. There are a lot of things like that in England. It isn't cricket to complain. If you get cheated at poker, left out at golf, over-handicapped at billiards, or sandbagged on the street – if your broker makes off with your money, and your friend runs away with your wife – you don't say anything. It's not cricket.

So the further you look into the problem of the sport, the more perplexing it becomes. But after all is said and done you feel there must be *something* in it. Out of this queer figure, with a check waistcoat and a loud tie, drinking snifters for manliness and taking a cricket ball in the stomach for the game's sake, emerges a kind of something that we would all like to be. Civilization has patterned and stamped us into its mould till each is much like each and lives as the others do. But embedded in each of us is a sort of original man, a higher cast of being, that in moments of danger and emergency takes control, and flames out into something far beyond our wonted range.

It may be that the "sport," who is in all of us to a certain degree, is a sort of pale reflection of this superman. For the sport, after all, never complains – if he's sick with his snifters, he doesn't say so; if he's afraid, he mustn't say so; and if he wears a loud tie, it is only from a humble sense that without a loud tie he wouldn't be loud enough – just as a savage paints his face to make himself look savage.

Oh, yes. I guess a sport is all right. Here's to him – have a snifter.

Why Do We Fish?

The Complete Philosophy of the Angler

THIS ARTICLE is intended to put the reader to sleep, put him fast asleep – in a motor boat anchored out on the still water of a still lake on one of those stillest days of the summer, at the drowsiest hour of the day . . . fast asleep, his hat fallen over his eyes, his line dangling in the water, but with a magazine across his lap to show that his brain made a fight for it.

Everybody who goes bass-fishing in a motor boat on such waters as our Canadian lakes in midsummer knows of this drowsy hour. No one admits its existence. No one acknowledges that he ever falls asleep. But the fact is there. So the best way is to carry along "something to read" – and then not read it.

This bringing things "just in case" is quite in accordance with fishing standards. It is wise always to pack a lunch (and not eat it), or carry a flask – no, that's the exception that proves the rule. But every fisherman ought to carry along something to read – so as not to read it. You see, if you didn't have it you might wish you had something to read, and if you do, then you don't – see? It's not very clearly explained but I am sure you understand. So, as I say, it's well to have something along in a motor boat for the browsing hour. Some men use a magazine but others think a better thing is a list of the votes in the presidential election, state by state, since 1788. Another good thing, if you can get hold of it, is the agricultural statistic abstract of the United States. That's grand reading for a summer's day. Such things help to make the proper environment, the peculiar detachment from the world that is the real charm of fishing.

Let it be understood right away that real fishermen don't go fishing for the sake of the fish. They pretend they do. It is a good excuse for paying ten dollars for a new rod and five dollars for a new reel to say that after all fishing cuts down housekeeping bills. Not at all. No true fisherman ever wants to eat the darned things. At the close of the day he tries to give them to the other fellows. They won't take them. He tries to give them to the guide. But the guide has plenty; he compromises on a cigar. It ends with sending the fish in a basket to a friend – especially to a clergyman. In my part of the country the clergymen eat little else all summer.

To me, as to ever so many other people, there is a singular and abiding charm about fishing. I began it as a little boy, fishing below a mill-dam in the roar and foam of the water. Now, as an old man, I fish above the dam. It's quieter there. That's all the difference.

And of course I admit that I only know of fishing on a somewhat limited and humble scale – I know nothing, for example, of the "Big stuff" of salmon fishing. In that, I gather, you throw a fly into the mouth of a salmon in the middle of a boiling river, then let out half a mile of line, then run hard half a mile downstream passing the salmon as it runs up and so on back and forwards. You do that up and down. It's called landing the salmon. An expert can take half a day at it. Nor do I know anything – or rather I know all I want to, for ever – of fishing in the real Canadian wilderness where you stay out for three days at a time and catch so many bass the first evening before sundown that the next day you just throw the fish back, and the next day you play poker and the third day go home a day before you have to.

My fishing is beside a mill-dam, or the remains of what once was one, a place with old beams and fragments of machinery sticking out in the wreckage of a bygone mill; there or along the banks of the stream that feeds the pond; or better still in a motor boat on a lake that is neither wilderness nor civilization, neither multitude nor solitude, with enough bass in it to keep hope alive and not enough to make continuous trouble. For fishing, as I see it, is in reality not so much an activity as a state of mind.

I can give you an idea of what I mean about the peculiar tranquility, this peculiar atmosphere of fishing, by speaking of a little episode of two or three years ago – yes, the year before the war – on one of my Lake Simcoe motor-boat fishing days. There were half a dozen of us in the boat, and one was just out from England, an English crime story writer and lecturer. He was fascinated, as everyone is at first sight, with the kind of scene, the beautiful clear water and winding channels and the island near the shore, and the clear, open lake with just the breath of ripples wafted over it in moving patches here and there.

Yet being a crime writer, our visitor carried his trade with him all day. He couldn't help it. After we had been out two or three hours he said to me, "Do you know this gives me a great idea for a detective story – absolutely new setting."

"Tell me about it," I said. I saw no way to stop him.

"Why," he said, "in a way it's the ordinary type of story where you get six or seven people isolated and there's a murder and one of them *must* have done it, because there have been no other people there."

"Yes," I said, "I know the kind of story. You have to sort them all out one by one."

"Exactly. One of them has committed the murder but the difficulty is, which? Then just as they're speculating and suspecting one another, there's a second murder, see?"

"Yes," I said, "I know the type."

"All right – but the point is that I'd put them on a boat like this, this kind of party – and after they have been out about an hour one is missing – then a little later another . . . think of the rising horror of it . . . and then presently a third . . . a perfect agony of fear! See? The way I'm going to work it will be that the hired man who runs the boat – like *him*, there, what's his name, Jake? – you know –"

"A dipsomaniac?" I suggested; that's the worst I can think of any fisherman.

"No, no, a monomaniac, a criminal monomaniac. You see you start out with the beautiful, peaceful setting; then you gradually build up the horror. As each new one disappears, don't you see, the horror deepens . . ."

"My dear fellow!" I said. "There wouldn't be any horror. It just shows you don't understand fishing. Let me explain to you how it would happen. Suppose it happened to us. We'll imagine that we have been out half an hour or so, clean away from the dock and down the narrows and just out on the lake when some one – we'll say the doctor there . . ."

"What's that?" said the doctor from his seat in the stern end. "Did you get a bite?"

"No, no," I said. "I was just saying suppose you were murdered."

"Oh, all right. I thought you had a bite."

"Well," I continued to my guest, "you see, some one would say, 'Where's the doctor?' and everybody would look up; and somebody else would say, 'I certainly saw him on the dock, he certainly came in his car.' Then there would be an awkward silence; it's hard to give up a day's fishing. Somebody would say: 'I guess he got off the boat again. The doctor got off the boat again, didn't he, Jake?'

"Jake would turn round from his steering wheel. 'I think he did,' he says. Jake agrees with everybody. He used to be a bar-tender.

"Then an hour later," I continued, still talking with the guest, "another one would suddenly have disappeared. Of course this time he couldn't have stayed on the dock. So when some one says suddenly, 'Where's Charlie Janes?' there is a mighty uncomfortable moment. It looks as if the fishing were spoilt after all. But luckily some one says, 'Didn't Charlie get off the boat to fish on the big rock beside Grape Island?' – 'Yes! he must have. We left him behind but we can pick him up on the way back!' It's thin of course, but when some one else says, 'Hold on, I've got a bite,' the second disappearance passes off. Then a little later one man would whisper to the one next him, 'I'm afraid George has fallen overboard.' The other would nod and whisper back, 'All right.' We'll now admit that it gets down to two – just two left with Jake, and by that time the day would be pretty well over. So one would say, 'Look here, Jake, you can't work this thing on us any more. You've thrown three of our friends into the lake. On the other hand we've had a real good day's fishing and are not inclined to make too much of it. You can head back for the dock, Jake, but we're certainly not going to pay anything for the boat.' 'That's fair enough,' Jake would say and the mystery would fade out into the idea that they swam home – the atmosphere of the evening would melt all the horror out of it like bees-wax. Did you ever use bees-wax for a bamboo rod?"

That's the way I argued it out with this English story writer. But the odd thing was the peculiar sequel, which came near making a real story out of it. I wish I could tell a lie – I mean in print – and stretch the point a little, but anyway what happened was pretty close to it.

It had grown dusk, too dark to see decently, and we were just getting ready to pull up the lines and the English visitor was standing up fishing over the stern of the boat, a silly thing to do on the smooth convex hardwood decks they put on them now. Anyway as the boat started forward, he fell off into the lake in the dark. . . Yes, I admit we picked him up; that's the pity of it. It would have been a fine story if we hadn't. Especially as we didn't notice him for a minute. I said to the doctor, "Where's our friend?" and he said, "Up forward," and I said, "Are you sure?" and he said, "Quite . . ." Then the motor stalled, or something; anyway we got him. Hard luck, wasn't it?

But at least it illustrates the point, the peaceful atmosphere, fishing – good will towards man, eh?

When Fellers Go Fishing

IF I WERE writing this discussion as a scientific essay, I should put as the title, *The Reaction of Fishing upon the Psychology of the Individual*. That would guarantee that no one would read it. But if I label it as above, "*When Fellers Go Fishing*," that enlists the sympathy of everybody, at least that is, off everybody who matters – all the people who go fishing.

From time immemorial, fishing has had this peculiar, sympathetic claim. King James spoke of fishing as "the apostles' own calling." And long before King James, in the earliest twilight of our literature, in all old tales and legends, a fisherman was supposed to be a kindly fellow, poor but likeable, whereas a merchant was a cheat, and a lawyer, when he presently appeared, stood for a crook. It was always a poor fisherman who found an emerald in the belly of a fish, a poor fisherman to whom a Saint appeared, or a poor fisherman who saved a little drowning maiden who turned out to be a princess. Think what a thrill of interest Charles Kingsley gives us in his famous poem that begins, "Three fishers went sailing, out into the west." But suppose he had said, "Three lawyers took the train to the east." Not the same at all. Even now, when the writer of a crime story wants to indicate that one of the characters concerned must be all right at heart, he describes him as "passionately fond of angling." It is to be observed that "angling" is the name given to fishing by people who can't fish.

Now here is why fishing has this peculiar appeal. In the far-away past, fishing played a far larger part in human life, inconceivably larger, than it does now. It outdates agriculture by centuries. All of the people from whom we descend lived beside and on the waters. In each of us is buried, thirty generations down, the soul of a bygone fisherman. And our city office men, when you take them away from their desks and get them out with the sound of the waves and the song of the wind in their ears, turn back again into fishermen. "I've never been out fishing before," says such a one as the motor boat bears him out on the lake, the tackle and gear all stowed and ready for the day's work. What, never before? Yet look at the queer far-away look that comes into his eye, turning to the horizon, seeking back unconsciously the lost memories of a thousand years ago. What, never before? Why, have you forgotten how you and I went fishing off the coast of what we now call Norway, in the days of Hengist and Horsa? That's what you're listening for, my dear sir, the sound of the waves beating on the broken shoals among which our great boat with its single sail is driving. Sounds like these still echo in the ears of infant children, before the age of speech and conscious memory. The child that stirs and murmurs in its sleep is hearing the waves of the North Sea, and calling to you to pull hard on the steering oar, to keep the boat from the breakers.

Mere fancy this? Imagination? Not at all, plain scientific fact. Ask any biologist and he'll tell you that it's plain truth, only he'll use such a maze of scientific terms that he'll take all the simple meaning out of it. He'll admit that the "ichthyological impulse is part of our Mendelian heritage" – then he will pause and correct his statements by saying that perhaps "piscatorial urge" would be a better term that "ichthyological impulse." So you can have your choice. What he really means is that every man, deep down, is a fisherman.

So when people go out fishing, or are taken out fishing, this "piscatorial urge" gets hold of them. You know what is meant by "atavism," by "throwing back" to the characters of far-away ancestors. Well, that is what they get. The transformation is best seen – and this is in accordance with scientific law – is best seen in the case of beginners, of people doing a thing for the first time with only instinct to guide them. Observe this man whom you have asked out for a day's fishing – what did you say he was by profession? A stock-broker. Oh, yes – ! well, he's looking through his clothes cupboard for a suit to wear out fishing. Don't interrupt him, don't disturb him. He knows better than you what he wants. He's looking for that old suit of tanned leather that he wore in the North Sea, a thousand years ago. Hush, let him look – there! He's found it. I admit that what you see, or think you see, is the old pair of ginger-brown pants that the tailor cut too big by accident and that his wife has tried to throw away a dozen times already – but what *he* sees is a suit of seal-hide that he wore when his name was Lief Hellslinger, and he smashed through the foam off the Faroe Islands.

That is why when you take men out fishing they turn up in such queer costumes. Here's one with a red coat on and a red knotted band round his waist – old junk from his snow-shoeing days very likely – but to him it's the stuff he wore as a Carthaginian fisherman off the coast of Tunis in the days of Hannibal. See the feller with the huge rubber boots (a plumber left them in his cellar) he wears those, though he doesn't know it, so that an octopus can't bite him.

This is the deep hidden reason why a party of "fishermen" always look so queer. The stores try to make these things but they can't. Patent rubber jackets and Norfolk coats with side flap pockets, and pancake waterproof hats – oh, no! you can spend a couple of hundred dollars on this stuff and all you look like is an American millionaire who has rented a Scottish salmon stream – you've seen him in pictures a hundred times. Beside him, by the way, is a Scottish "gillie" – the real thing – with clothes that go back to the Picts and Scots of the Emperor Hadrian's time.

As with the transformation of clothes, so with the transformation of character. It seems to me that men out fishing take on, as it were, a new character, or at least resurrect one buried long ago and lost under the surface of daily life. I spoke a moment ago of the transformation of my friends when out fishing – bass fishing for example – in a motor boat on one of our lakes where they turn back into Saxons of the North Sea. But take the same men out fishing on a river stream "out in the bush" nicely out of the beaten path of highways and civilized meals, and they'll turn back further still. They'll go clear back to the ancient Britons in the woods – suddenly become ingenious, subtle, silent, full of wood-craft. When you see such a man go into the bush you realize that it is a pity he ever came out of it. Watch him squatting beside the fire that he is managing to make burn out of wet twigs in a drizzling rain. The ground is sodden. Does he know it? The smoke puffs in his eyes. Does he feel it? No, of course not – this man is clean back to the days of Boadicea; after three days in the bush he'll tan as dark as an Iberian Celt; he'll be stained with woad (from his cigarettes) and he'll eat a pound and a half of meat at a sitting, and be out at sunrise, fishing in the foam below a fall. Stand it? Why, he can stand anything! Yet, this is the same man that last week was breakfasting on half a grapefruit with bromo-seltzer, who sent the waiter to tell the head waiter to tell the management of the hotel that the room was chilly, and who could quarrel and get angry over a trifle, or a misstatement, a contradiction, that out fishing he couldn't hear and wouldn't notice if he did.

Quarrels, arguments! – no, that's another thing about fishing. There's no room, no time for that. A little genial discussion, if you will, as to whether a gut leader on a bass line is any good, or no damn good. That's all right, that's science. But to think of quarreling over the things men argue about in ordinary life – such as whether Sir John A. Macdonald died in 1891 or 1892: whether John L. Sullivan was born in Ireland, and whether the Scott Act came first, or Local Option!

Oh, no, a man fishing is too broad-minded to dispute over these things. What does that matter? And anyway you can't hear what the other fellow is saying for the noise of the fall. Look, Ed's got another over there. "Attaboy, Ed! only darn it, he can't hear."

But remember – just one last caution. After you have been out with a "bunch" of darned good fellows for four days on the Maganetawan, or in the bush country north of Lake Nipigon – don't – no, very particularly don't – ask that group of men to come and all dine together at your club in the city on their return. If you do, you'll find that the magic has all gone! There they are! – not a bunch, but a group – back in their little Tuxedo jackets, shaved each as pink as a dressed hog, precise, formal – and eating like sick hens pecking damaged grain. The magic is all gone! The enchantment has vanished, as enchantment always does, vanished and gone over night. The North Sea, and the Carthaginians and the Britons squatting beside the smoky fire – oh, no, those are not these men. . . . Maid, will you tell the steward, we've been waiting five minutes already for our coffee!

Eating Air

A Discourse on the Magic of Eating Out of Doors

I WANT IN this article to talk about eating in the open air – about the joy and exhilaration of it, about the health of it. I'm enthusiastic about it. I'm crazy over it and have been for years. I think that eating in the open air – which really means "eating air" – is the greatest tonic, stimulant, restorative – I can't think of enough words for it, but those will give a first idea.

I'm so enthusiastic about it that I'd like to get out in the street and talk about it, under a naphtha lamp on the street corner in the evening, with just a little table with a beefsteak pie on it, and I'd say: "Oh, friends, I want you to gather round this evening and watch me eat this pie!" And then: "And, oh, dear friends, I want you all to go and get a pie of your own (not mine) and take it away and eat it somewhere in the open, somewhere in the great spaces, in the woods, out in a sail-boat on a lake, or in some snug corner of rock and sand beside the sea."

Or I'd like, if I may put the imagery another way, to be a spirit and appear in the office of a business man, one of the kind called executives, who can't digest anything and live on toast. I'd be a spirit and I'd appear in his office just about one o'clock. He could see me but no one else could. His stenographer couldn't see me – though, of course, I could see her – oh, certainly. Anyway I'd appear and I'd say, "I want to take you out to lunch." And he'd look up and say, "To lunch, where?" And I would whisper in his ear, "Below the mill-dam!" He'd say, "What!" and I'd say: "Close your eyes and listen! Call back the picture of the snug corner among the broken stones just below the mill-dam, close to the roar and foam of the water, where you used to fish when you were a boy. That's where you always ate the packet of lunch you carried in your pocket, there on a pile of rocks and the broken debris of an old mill . . . well, that's where we're going to eat. Come along; you don't need a hat."

So come, my dear reader, close *your* eyes, come along with me, and we'll call up in fancy some of the ways and places of eating in the open air. . . . I'll tell you what I'll do; I'll take you out fishing in my sail-boat and we'll eat lunch right on the boat, as we always do, with the boat at anchor with about a hundred feet of cable out and just enough sea running to make her lift to it a little. There is a fresh breeze blowing – just fresh enough so that it's snug to keep out of it and yet you can't quite keep out of it. . . .

You notice those terms, the "cable" and the "sea." That's the nautical touch. The "cable" means the anchor rope and the "sea" is those little waves that are rocking the boat – well, they're not so darned little. And I always call the boat *she* unless I forget and call her *it*. She's the old-fashioned, heavy-built boat; sloop-rigged – none of your dinghy stuff – and it holds four (she does) just nicely, one on the starboard side pretty well forward, one abeam to port and two abaft in the lee-scuppers. (I'm sorry if you don't get all that; one sits each side of the centre-board and two on the broad backseat.)

So now, that's enough for the forenoon's fishing. We didn't get any fish yet though we lost a beauty. Anyway, it's time to eat. Time? Oh, boy, is it time? Well, I'll say so. . . . Yet only half an hour ago, when I asked, "What about lunch?" you answered, "Oh, not for hours yet!" . . . But now, let's get to it . . . turn that sideflap up and it makes a table over the centre-board . . . that's it . . . now, haul out those boxes from under the forward deck and we'll unpack them. . . . What have we here? There's a cold beef-steak pie, with the whole rattle of plates and knives and forks that go with it. . . . Yes, unroll that; that's a ham, or rather half a ham, because I find that with only four of us if we have a beef-steak pie we only need half a ham, I mean if we have a cold chicken. . . . We may eat the cold chicken or we may not, but I like to see a cold chicken all rolled up in a napkin with lettuce leaves almost as pale as itself . . . looks nice, doesn't it? All right, just cut me a piece while I get the bottles of beer out. . . .

Not that I mean to imply that on my boat we go in for anything elaborate, still less for anything gluttonous . . . never too much, is the rule. In years and years on the boat I have never had too much to eat and drink; can't get it. We generally take just the plain stuff I've mentioned – a meat pie, a ham and a cold chicken and with that a plain salad already mixed in a bowl with plenty of hard-boiled eggs in it – bread in plain rolls, always a bottle of mixed pickles and the little things like salt and pepper and a bottle of sauce, and that's the whole of it except the cheese and perhaps a little fruit, and to drink (apart from a nip of whisky before lunch) bottled ale or, for those who don't drink bottled ale, bottled beer.

There! let's sit down and eat. Here, take this napkin. Napkins? Why, of course! I like to have them, large and big and white as snow – they give a touch to lunch on a boat. There: tuck your legs in beside the centre-board – or, all right, if you like, take your plate and stuff up forward on the half-deck . . . now, say when!

Tastes good? Doesn't it! Digest it? – Why, my dear sir,

with that fresh air blowing into you, you could digest a chunk of sandstone rock. . . .

You see, if I may interrupt myself to say it again, the point is, not that you are eating in the open air but that you are actually *eating air*. As every chemist (every good one) knows, air is made up of equal parts of oxygen, hydrogen, nitrogen, iron and alcohol, with just a little touch of the rarer elements argol, and golgol, though these last were only found a few years ago. Now, these are the very things that support life, and these are what is found in fresh air. Only the air must be fresh. The ordinary indoor air that you breathe is filled with dust, feathers, dried ink, powdered leather – heaven knows what. You need only to let a full streak of sunlight break into a room to see what the air in it contains. Now when you're out in the open, in the straight clear open, you're breathing the pure oxygen, taking in argol and alcohol with every breath. Look at people who live in the open. Have you ever seen one of those ruddy-looking Highland gillies who spend their days on the wind-swept moor and the open braes and breeks? You haven't! Well, neither have I, but I've seen the pictures of them, in the Scotch whisky advertisements. What makes them ruddy? What makes them live till they die? The fresh air, the alcohol.

But don't let me seem to imply that eating in a sail-boat out fishing is the only kind of eating in the open air. There are ever so many others. My friends who go out duck-hunting tell me that food never tastes so good as the snack of breakfast they carry in a side-pocket, to eat when out in the early morning. You go out, as you know, just about day-break or a little before, so that the ducks don't know you're there, and you stand in the dark in a marsh among the reeds and wait patiently till the ducks fly over, and then – bang! bang! – you've missed them, but that doesn't matter. The point is, so I am credibly assured, that no home breakfast ever tastes so good as the snack you eat just about sun-up – a cold sausage with a jam roll, washed down with a little gin and marshwater. A man who, in his club, couldn't eat a chicken-patty-à-la-Reine without getting melancholy with indigestion, who gets heavy after lunch, soggy after dinner and dull all day, can get out in a marsh and eat a chunk of cold bologna that would choke a cannibal – yes, and feel bright and happy over it, and think the world a fine place. Bang! missed another duck by talking so much.

But much better – and this is one of my own – try eating lunch, individual lunch, along a trout stream; carry it with you on your hip, and let each of the other fellows do the same. That's the way I do on my stream. I have rights along about three miles of a little river that runs among woods and fields and over banks, stones and around corners, diving under fallen trees and sunken logs – hurrying on to nowhere, and always as cold and clear as when it started. I am lucky enough to have "rights" (not trout, *rights*) on about three miles of this. It's like all other trout streams. There *used* to be a tremendous lot of trout there. So there *must* be some now. But we won't go into that. Anyway, for fishing of that sort the individual lunch is the thing – just a neat packet done up in oiled paper – cold chicken sandwiches – that kind of thing. Of course, it's not enough. . . . That's the point of it. But Oh, my! how good it tastes, eaten as you sit on a big rock beside a pool in the river. . . . That, with a dash of cold clear water from the stream itself. I am so keen personally on cold water that I always like to supply each of my fishing guests with a good cut-glass tumbler to carry along with him – no scooping up the water with his hands, or with the greasy-looking "cup" of a flask – no, sir, clear cut-glass, clean as crystal and the water sparkling in it, fresh from its river bed! . . . There, hold it steady and pour in just enough whisky to preserve the clarity of the water. How much? well, there's the point. Be careful . . . not *too* much or you'll spoil it . . . and not too little, or that fails to bring out the clarity of the water. But after all it's very simple. If you have too much whisky put in more water, then try if it's right, and if you get it a little wrong the other way put in more whisky. If you keep trying it out with a little more of each every time, you'll soon get it.

I know that some readers might object that eating in the open air is all right but ask why I connect it with the rough stuff – pounding up and down in a sail-boat or standing in a stream? The answer is that you don't have to. Eating air is eating air, and if you like you can eat it with as much luxury and comfort as ever you want. For instance, on my trout stream we don't always have lunch in the way I have described. Sometimes, when I want to do the thing properly, I have a prearranged general lunch at a fixed hour, with a real table made up, and all sorts of things.

Of course, when I do this I have to take a "man" along – I mean that, apart from the half-dozen men that I have asked to fish, I take along a "man" to fix the table and do all that. I am sure that everybody knows that rather perplexing use of the word "man." You've often heard a woman say that for such and such a thing round the house that her husband couldn't do, she had to get a "man." Every married woman knows that a husband just goes so far. After that you have to get a "man."

Well, in the same way, when I want to do things up in style I take along a man. And my man, who is an old soldier, is a most handy fellow. Take him out that way, leave him under a shady tree and wander off up the stream for a couple of hours fishing and then come back and, there! look! There's a whole table with seats somehow rigged up under the tree, with a cloth spread over it and an array of bottles and dishes and plates and things half seen, half hidden, ends of green cucumbers peeping out from beneath a napkin – and at the side – well, I'm darned! – an improvised ice-box! – ale on the ice! – cocktails cooling! – Oh, boy! – life in the woods for me.

And at such a table you can eat and eat; never mind your digestion, you can't get heavy if you try. Have some more cucumber, they're light as froth. . . . Because, you see, and I can't repeat it too often, you are eating *air*. I mean literally and physically eating it with your food, actually taking in all those things the argol, the gargoyles, the oxygen. The air that you eat with them breaks them up into vitamins. . . .

I wish I were scientist enough to explain it physically. I once asked a professor of physics how it stood, and he said that you could put the thing very simply mechanically. He said that a man's stomach is practically a sphere – I admit that some look it – and that from a very elementary formula we know that its volume is exactly four thirds of a little over three times half the distance across his stomach cubed. This means that like all spheres it expands equally in all directions provided the pressure is constant and uniform. Well, there you are! When you eat out of doors it *is*. So you can eat all you like.

But some one might say I have talked only of eating cold food out of doors and left out all question of cooking in the open – left out, some people would say, the finest part of it. Don't I know it? But it's only through sheer lack of time and space. Cooking out of doors – over a fire made in the bush! How I would like to give a whole lecture on it! I'd like to get the Pope and the Archbishop of Canterbury and the Librarian of Congress – I mean people who always live indoors – and take them out into the Canadian bush and cook them a steak! My! Wouldn't they be surprised when I showed them that the point is that you don't make a big fire but a *little* fire! I'd like the Pope to watch while I laid down two small logs side by side. I'd like the Archbishop to say,

"But, surely, the logs are rather too *green* to burn!" And I say: "No, no, *you* are; ask the Pope; I want the logs green so that they *won't* burn." Now, watch me cook the steak. See it jump; see those ashes falling into the pan? – That's what puts the taste in – excuse me, I must upset it once. Now, Pope, you're the senior, here's yours. Eat it on a shingle. . . . Now watch me boil the tea. . . . Yes, boil it – the only way to make real tea, boiled from the cold water up. . . . But stop, the Archbishop wants more steak.

So there the topic is – real as real, and one of the greatest things in the world. *Eat more air*, never mind vitamins. The air is full of them. *Eat the air*. Take it in with every bite, break it into every morsel. . . .

Tell the doctors about it? You don't need to. They know it. Don't you know that every doctor, the moment he gets a few days off, beats it for the bush? Any time you go into the rough country, in the bush and round the lakes, you find it full of doctors, eating steaks beside a log. . . . But you'd hardly expect them to bring their patients.

Studies in Humour

The Saving Grace of Humour

Is There Any?

NOW ESPECIALLY, in the distress of war, the familiar reference is made to the saving grace of humour as a consolation in adversity. But I am afraid there's not much in it – I doubt if any saving grace of humour can help us – at any rate not against personal discomfiture.

I recall here, from years back, once hearing an academic colleague of mine say, "Thank Heaven, I can fall back on my sense of humour." He was speaking with the quivering, ruffled dignity of a professor – you know what they're like – after some little academic tiff or dispute, a small, precise man, myopic, over-polite and sensitive as a mimosa plant. "In fact," he added, "I can even afford to laugh about it, ha! ha!"; and he gave an imitation of a man laughing an easy, careless laugh – as nearly as he could register it. If he had a sense of humour I never saw it; he never seemed to get any nearer to it than telling long stories about Talleyrand, at professors' dinner parties. You know the kind. But yet he carried with him the idea that he could always fall back on his sense of humour – like throwing himself into a firemen's net.

Strange, isn't it?, how we always try to have some refuge of this sort, something to fall back upon. An old friend of mine once told me he could always fall back on his classical education. I'd as soon fall back on a cucumber frame as on mine. Other people fall back on their family. "After all," I heard a mother say to her son, "you can always remember you're an O'Brien." Personally I could see no consolation in that, except that it was easier than trying to remember you were an O'Flaherty.

But so it is, in our sorely beset pilgrimage; we like to have something to fall back upon – a second line of retreat from the slings and arrows. And the belief is familiar, that this refuge can be found in a sense of humour.

The world loves to read stories of how humour sustains people in moments of emergency and in the supreme hour. Thus it is told of the aged Sir Thomas More, beheaded by Henry VIII, that as he went up the steps of the scaffold he leaned on the executioner with the words, "I pray you give me your aid in my going up; as for my coming down I can make shift for myself." It is told of him, presumably on the same occasion, that as he laid his head on the block he moved aside his snow-white beard, "Pity to cut that," he said; "that has not committed treason." In fact the only trouble with these Thomas More stories is that there are getting to be too many of them. Where did I read one the other day that said: Every time that Sir Thomas More was executed he used to have a clean shave. "Pity," he said, "to get my beard spoiled." I felt when I read it that there was something wrong with that story, though it's hard to see just what. Or was it an advertisement, that read: Sir Thomas More said, "I know nothing like Silver-Glass soap; nothing like it for a hasty shave before execution." But I doubt whether in reality Sir Thomas More got much consolation or fun out of any of it. The executioner probably got more than he did. "Certainly," said the executioner, laughing as he swung up the axe, "you are the most humorous gentleman I ever –" chuck!

Such stories of humour in the presence of death, don't go. Here is Rabelais, for example, saying "I am about to take a leap into the great perhaps!" And here is the story of O. Henry's last hour on which those of us who love his writings have lingered with wistful affection. "Turn up the light," he said, as the room darkened; "I don't want to go home in the dark." Yet this is not humour. This is pathetic, tragic; this is just the mind still functioning in a worn groove, reverting back like Falstaff when he "babbled of green fields." The cold reality of death cannot be exorcised with a joke. . . .

But if you want to see death and danger treated with absolutely unconcerned laughter turn back again to the stories of adventure that you used to read when you were a boy. Open again the pages of *Ned Dashaway*, or *Adventures on the Spanish Main*. See where it reads: *"Warm work, Ned," laughed Captain Bilge, as a volley of grape cleared three men out of the main top. "It certainly is," roared Ned, as a volley of cannister swept the bosun and four men off the main-deck. "I'll say so too," chuckled the mate, as a round shot bowled him into the lee-scuppers.*

You notice in these stories, now that you can look at them with the eye of experience, that to keep up the laugh they have to avoid all gruesome details of blood and butchery. What happened to the men in the main top? – They got cleared out of it – that's all – and only cleared with "grape"! That's nothing – and the bosun and his crowd? They got swept off the deck. No harm in that – just a sort of "Excuse me, gentlemen, we want to sweep this deck." Reality is very different from that.

Do you remember how good old Mark Twain wrote a book that he called *Joan of Arc* and really thought was Joan of Arc, and wanted to bring in mediaeval hand-to-hand fighting; and he couldn't do it – unconsciously, I mean, he couldn't. He tried to and it came out like this, in a passage meant to describe a fierce and bloody assault: "We had a long and tough piece of work before us, but we carried it through before night, Joan keeping us hard at it."

Kept them *hard at it*, eh? spirited girl. It sounds like a Missouri paring bee. No, no, there is no humour in the realities of emergency, danger and death.

Nor can I feel that it could in any way soften or redeem the character of bloodthirsty and awful people if they showed a high sense of humour. If I have to think of Ivan the Terrible, I'd rather think of him as Terrible and let it go at that; I don't want him funny. I'd rather take Blackbeard the pirate as straight Blackbeard and not understand that though he made people walk the plank he could always enter into the fun of the thing. I wouldn't think any better of Bluebeard if I heard that he used to roar over the *Pickwick Papers*. This is the principle on which are based those masterpieces of humour, the *Ruthless Rhymes* of the late Captain Harry Graham. The humour of them lies in the ridiculous incongruity as between the actual tragedy and the cheerful unconcern of the spectators. In other words the saving grace of humour, produced, like the parallel lines of Euclid, "ever so far both ways," reveals its weakness by failing to meet. Readers who know the Rhymes already will forgive me for quoting an example:

> My son Augustus in the street one day
> Was feeling quite particularly merry,
> When some one asked him, "What's the quickest way
> To get me out to Highgate Cemetery?"
> "The quickest way?" replied my little Gus,
> And pushed the feller underneath a bus.
> I will say this about my son,
> He does enjoy a bit of fun.

But in reality when tragedy steps in, humour moves out. It is too soft a plant, too soft a blossom for such a soil. Humour springs best from happiness, bubbles forth with the champagne around the festive board. A jail is no place for it. It belongs either with happiness, or with the remembrance of bygone happiness, or with that long retrospect into a past so far away that the pain is out of it. "Battles long ago" are different. I can laugh at Jack and the Giant Killer and the Welsh Giant . . . but that's far away.

Yet I admit we have to make a pretense at humour in moments of trial. It is a sort of survival quality that came down with us through the ages that we must take adversity with a smile or a joke. Tell any man that he has lost his job, and his "reaction," as they say in college, will be to make some kind of joke about having lots of time now for golf. In each of us is the dim conception of being a "sport," a survival, I do not doubt, of bygone ages when of necessity courage was the highest virtue. So it is that collectively and singly we still keep up a brave little show of "laughing it off!" of "clink to the Cannikin, clink!" – a whole repertory of little verses saying that we don't care – when our hearts are broken. . . . Yet this is not humour; this is courage that makes a pretense of it.

I spoke of the *Pickwick Papers*, written, as I am sure some one interrupted to remind me, nearly a hundred years after Blackbeard's death. Now there, I admit, that's different. This is humour not as a saving grace for the maker of it, but handed out as salvation, or at least consolation for mankind. All Dickens's humour couldn't save Dickens, save him from his overcrowded life, its sordid and neurotic central tragedy and its premature collapse. But Dickens's humour, and all such humour, has saved or at least greatly served the world.

One thinks of the *Pickwick Papers* – read in all corners of the world, in the loneliness of exile, in the vigil of the sickroom, in the pauses of toil and the breathing spaces of anxiety, and bringing with it at least a respite of escape, a vision of the lanes and hawthorns of England, of the Christmas snow, and the dim sound on the ear of the bugles of coaches. Nothing else is read like that. Civilization's best legacy, thus far, is the world's humour.

In fact on reflection I'll go a little further in regard to this saving grace of humour. It helps to supply for us, in its degree, such reconciliation as we can find for the mystery, the sorrows, the shortcomings of the world we live in, or, say, of life itself. Consolation is hard to find. You recall perhaps the haunting verses, written years ago, that ran, "There, little girl, don't cry." They have broken her dolls, yes, and later on, it will be her heart that is broken, but, "there little girl, don't cry." It is all that we can say to one another.

Now humour in its highest reach turns on just such feeling as this. It is not funny. It no longer rests on quips of language, the oddities of situation or the incongruities of character – but on the incongruity of life itself. The contrast between the eager fret and anxiety of today, the angers that pass and are forgotten and in retrospect, like children's quarrels, provoke only a smile – this is the basis on which the world's greatest books of humour appeal to us. This mellowed vision even though not interpretation at least contains reconciliation and consolation.

Not that I mean that a person with a sense of humour can sit and chuckle over it all. That is given only to idiots. You can't slap your leg and roar with laughter at how funny it is the Romans are all dead. But at least – well – there's an idea that I am groping for, but as Sir Thomas More would say to the executioner, "Pity to spoil it."

Laughing Off Our History

As I said in the chapter above, it does not seem to me that there is any particular saving grace of humour as applied by the individual to his own fortunes. A humorous person, I think, would be apt to be cut more nearly to the heart by unkindness, more deeply depressed by adversity, more elated by sudden good fortune, than a person with but little of that quick sense of contrast and incongruity which is the focus of the humorous point of view.

But what the individual cannot do the nation can – not only can, but does. As a nation we perpetually "laugh off our history," finding amusement in each phase that passes, oddity in every retreating custom and silliness in each forgotten craze. Our attitude to the past is one of mingled reverence and amusement. The good old times are either a heroic age or an amusing aberration, Valhalla or Vaudeville, as you care to see it. A knight in armour is funny to a child, curious to an antiquarian and inspiring to a poet. King Arthur's Knights of the Round Table were heroic to Tennyson and comic to Mark Twain.

Hence it is that all national history marks down, as it descends the decades, a track of bygone jests, the deep ruts of bygone humour. If other records of history failed we could find it here.

I am reminded of the familiar quotation: "Give me the making of the songs of a nation, and I care not who makes its laws." Just what that means I don't quite know, except that it has a fine sound. But I could see a lot of meaning in saying: "Let me hear the jokes of a nation and I will tell you what the people are like, how they are getting on and what is going to happen to them." Indeed the idea could be applied to all the world's history and followed down, from the jokes in Egypt about the graft on the contracts for the pyramids to the jokes on the New Deal of today.

Without going so far and without leaving North America, it occurs to me that one might reconstruct the reaction of the history of our North American Continent on its humour during the past forty or fifty years. Let us go back as far as the period of the "Gay Nineties," still within pretty easy memory, and to the period, a little dimmer, of the Eighties. Let me see, what was happening in the United States? Grover Cleveland, railroads, graft, trusts, octopuses, Populists with one brace southwest to northeast, Knights of Labour, farmers and more farmers and the South still sorrowing. America was just moving off the farm to the factory, from the rural town to the metropolitan city.

The city then was not made up of sky-scrapers and apartment buildings and residential flats superimposed ten stories high. It was all made up of boarding-houses. To make a city you had to have a "depot," a Main Street of shops, and then miles and miles of boarding-houses, to which went horse-cars with tinkling bells – cars warmed with straw. All people lived in boarding-houses – young people, too young to have homes; old people, too old to keep them; students burning midnight oil; store clerks as soon as they had regular jobs, and theatrical people whenever they hadn't.

So, of course, a whole lot of our current jokes of those days turned on the boarding-house; on the landlady (poor maligned soul); on the boarder who couldn't pay; on the food, the accommodations, and the warmth maintained by one stove-pipe that passed each room in turn like the knight's move in chess. Any people who recall those days will remember such jokes as: "Mr. Smith," said the landlady, "I'll just give you three days to pay your board in." "All right," said Mr. Smith, "I'll take Lincoln's Birthday, Washington's Birthday and the Fourth of July." Or this one: "Are you boarding now?" "No, only scantling."

Part of the standing boarding-house joke was the frequency of moving from one boarding-house to another. Here belongs the story, apocryphal or true, of Mark Twain being seen, in his San Francisco days, carrying under his arm a cigar box tied with a string.

"Buying cigars?" asked a friend.

"No," said Mark, "moving my room."

The essence of the story, at any rate, is not exaggerated. I can speak here from personal experience. During my student days, in Toronto, I lived in fourteen different boarding-houses (all marked now, no doubt with tablets – aspirin tablets –) and I moved so frequently that I had a special rate of 20 cents, instead of 25, with Crashley's Express. Notice "express" did not mean in those days "express company." "Crashley's Express" just meant a man and a horse. I forget which was Crashley. An expressman was not a huge fellow like a modern truckman. He was just a little shrimp of a man, but he used to put on his shoulder a trunk three cubic feet each way (you know what I mean) and carry it up to the top floor. In his mid-agony, the landlady would call: "Be careful with that trunk against the stove-pipe." You see, if he hit the pipe, the whole heating installation was dislocated.

But the boarding-house joke was only one of the kinds of jokes that marked the days when America was moving from the farm to the factory, from doing things by hand to doing things by machinery. We had a whole field of fun with a standard crop of jokes about laying carpets, putting up stove-pipes, and starting balky horses. Try this:

The horse standing outside the drug store refused to start. "Hold on," said the good-natured druggist, coming out of his store to the aid of the man tugging at the horse's bridle, "let me blow some of this powder in his ear. It's a new dodge." "Pouf!" went the druggist and away went the horse and buggy! His owner watched him to the sky-line. "Now blow some in mine," he said.

The picture when you think of it – the street dozing in the sunshine, the horses at the hitching posts, the low buildings and the disappearance of the Main Street over the horizon – the picture is that of a vanished world.

Change in transport, indeed, effected the first great changes that came over our humour as the new century opened. On the drowsy world of the horse and buggy broke the motor car – the horses reared and balked, the motor honked, a battle was engaged. And now, forty years later, you can look over the field that was and dig up jokes as they dig up steel cuirasses in Belgium. Here is a jest that dates the period:

"What shall I do," said the new driver, "if I meet a skittish horse?"

"Well, I tell you," said the expert, "you'd better stop the car and then stop the engine, and if the horse keeps on being skittish you'd better take the machine to pieces and hide it in the grass."

Presently this world of new transport, of rapid communication, of pictures that moved and wires that talked, went sweeping into the World War of 1914, and with that came, I will not say, "War Humour" for there is no such thing, but the humour in despite of war. For mankind, after the first wave of emotion, of anger, horror and fascination – mankind had to find humour to help forget the agonies of war or break under the strain of it. Far away, indeed, these War Jokes seem now – quite unknown to the generation that has risen up since.

Such humour to the mass of the people in America was as new as war itself. For the older wars, humour and all, had drifted into history. There had been the jokes of the Civil War – all long dead – jokes about army contractors, draft evaders and "contraband" negroes, done out in the quaint misspelling of the immortal Artemus Ward and of Orpheus C. Kerr. These, in 1914, lived on only as history.

The humours of the Spanish War had already faded. "When you hear those bells go ting-a-ling-a-ling." One recalls the verses about the Spanish ships and the snowballs in hell, or the jokes on the impecuniosity of Spain.

"Charge!" shouted the Spanish officer.

"No," answered the manager of the arms factory, "C.O.D."

All that came and went so quickly that there was no time to develop a school, or mode, of jest or a reaction from jest to bitterness. But compare the World War in relation to humour. Its earlier jokes turned on the organization and discipline of war, all new to the public, all different from civil life.

A private in camp called out to a passing figure in khaki, "Hey, Buddy, give me a match." Then he realized his mistake. "I beg your pardon, sir," he stammered, "I didn't see you were a general."

"That's all right," said the general; "luckily for you, I'm not a second lieutenant."

But presently there came the jokes that turned on the disillusionment, the world weariness bred of years of war, the sentiment of its futility, the question, "What price glory?"

Here is such a one, related, so it is recorded, by General Pershing:

A dilapidated soldier, his clothing in rags, a shoe missing, his head bandaged and his arm in a sling, was heard to mutter to himself as he shambled away: "I love my country, I'd fight for my country, I'd die for my country. But if ever this damn war is over I'll never love another country!"

The "saddened" smiles with which people tried to "laugh off" the war were followed by the barrage of jests with which the nation greeted prohibition. These cracked like machine-gun fire along the trenches of the vaudeville stage from New York to Los Angeles. The cherished right to drink, down and outlawed, entrenched itself behind the right to joke. A new language sprang up – speaking of speak-easies, boot-leggers, hijackers, and hip flasks – and a new set of jokes with it.

But here a new problem arose. Was it wicked to joke about prohibition? If it was law now, shouldn't it be illegal to make fun of it? In England, it has always been forbidden – by a taboo – to make fun of the King or of the Archbishop of Canterbury. In America, by a taboo with a kick behind it, it is equally forbidden to make fun of the President. You may make game of him but not fun of him. Of these three the Archbishop is now out of it. You can have all the fun with him you like. But the other two hold.

So, as I say, a lot of people claimed it was wicked to laugh at prohibition. And in any case the laugh threatened to monopolize too much of the field. A lot of theatres put prohibition jokes on the ban. The poor low comedian saw his livelihood cut off before he got it. Many of the newspapers cut out all jokes on drink and, most typical of all, writers of popular fiction and crime stories had to cut all boozing out of the narrative. The great detective, hitherto eating nothing but all to the good on drink, had to work on tea, and looked pretty sour on it.

Yet oddly enough, in earlier days, as every joke book shows from Artemus Ward to Mr. Dooley, drink had formed the chief subject of the American joke for half a century – men coming home tight, men too tight to come home, men wondering where home was; there was no end to it. Second only to it were the perennial jokes on quaint negroes, comic Irishmen and Scotchmen from Aberdeen. Some graduate research student should work it out into percentages of frequency or – no, if he did he would make it so dry that even drink wouldn't keep wet.

Then came the jokes on the failures of prohibition – open laughs with obvious meaning.

"Look at that man," said the lady at the window; "he's fallen down in the street; he must be drunk."

"How can he be drunk?" said her friend; "it's prohibition."

And after that came the jokes that spelled good-bye to prohibition, and it was all over.

But when that huge figure with the feet of clay toppled over, down fell another beside it. This was the colossus called "Big Business" – the American Image before which we had all bowed down, which founded colleges and held on the palm of its hand the little shrimps called Science, and Learning, and the Ministry. Business had taken everything over, and then down went business in the depression – like Humpty Dumpty. When it fell off the wall of Wall Street the outside world laughed. "Oh, yeah!" – and after that nobody said any longer, "A business man told me." And if any one said, "Business men think . . ." the interruption was, "Do they?"

Thus, in the saddened world of business disaster people try to "laugh off" the depression.

"My husband," said the professor's wife to the family lawyer, "has had a complete breakdown and must do absolutely nothing for six months. His old students want to help him. What would you suggest they might do?"

"They might buy him a seat on the Stock Exchange."

So there we sat in our Post-War world of the Thirties. It was really a Pre-War world but we didn't know it. We kept ourselves as merry as we could with the old perennial jokes – the negro has been Heaven's blessing to America – and the jokes of the hour on depression, hard times, Hitler's hair and Mussolini's hairlessness.

But did the subject of our humour really change through all these passing decades? No, not in its reality, but only in its latest embodiment. Mankind laughs at its troubles and jests at its oppressors. Children make fun of father, schoolboys laugh at their teacher, students at their professors and prisoners at their guards and turnkeys. Laughter is the last refuge of sorrow or oppression. Our new oppressions of the moment – Industrial Collapse, the War Danger and such – only stepped into the place of the old ones.

With which it suddenly occurs to me that I have left out the most perennial topic of all, one that in 1939 was running as strong as it was a hundred years before. Women! Did that graduate student counting up his percentages touch me on the elbow and whisper "women"? Why, of course, women, women – the second most important thing in the world and, like all its treasured possessions, the object at once of its flattery and its jests. Jokes on women! Here is change indeed!

Many people can look back with me from memory, and all from hearsay and reading, and recall the "comic" woman of the Eighties and the Nineties. Here was the Old Maid, that butt of jokes that never ended from the *Pickwick Papers* on. An "Old Maid" – any years over thirty made her that – wore curl papers and frilled pantalettes. You remember the one who wanted the conductor to stop the train at Poughkeepsie because she had to take a pill! There were thousands of Old Maid jokes. But she's getting her own back now all right, with a lip-stick and a vanity box and her pantalettes thrown away when she goes on a "necking party."

Comic women – they're all gone. Women are emancipated, they have all been sophisticated (a Victorian Old Maid would have denied that *she* ever had), and their emancipation is written broad across the pages of humorous literature. Where, now, is the Suffragette, and the Woman with the axe, the Temperance Woman, and, best of all, the Blue Stocking? A woman who learned anything out of a book was funny in those days; a girl at college must be an awful frump! Algebra! Good God!

But now, look and see. College girls – Oh! my! The public just eats them up! Here they are, in their "shorts," all over the funny pages, getting off their he-and-she jokes and leaning out of their dormitory windows. The blessed damozels who leaned out from the golden bars of heaven were not a patch on them. And their language!

He: "I love to think of you as the old-fashioned girl – sweet, beautiful, adorable, innocent."

She: "Yeah! Big boy, what kind of chump are you?"

How much has it all really changed, our humour? I only wish I had the time and space to talk about it. Believe me, fun didn't die with Mark Twain and Josh Billings. There are a lot of solemn people among us today, but so there were in Mark Twain's time. Pericles said – or let's be exact – Thucydides said Pericles said, "All the world is filled with the graves of brave men." Senator Tom Corwin – you've heard of him, from Ohio, long ago – improved on this and said, "All the world is filled with the graves of solemn jackasses."

They are still mooning round among us, and they get a sort of false admiration. But mainly we can laugh them off. For, after all, we still have our sense of humour and our jokes.

But while we were still making as merry as we could with Depression Jokes and College Girl Comics, all of a sudden – sudden for the honest people of the world – Depression, Collapse, jokes and all, were swept aside with the new tempest of war.

What price humour now?

War and Humour

I AM QUITE sure that when Adam and Eve were put out of the Garden of Eden, Eve said, "Well, thank goodness, Adam, we've got our sense of humour!" And Adam, trudging along deep in thought, paused and said, "How's that?" – and took a first step towards getting one. "I certainly had to laugh at that snake!" said Eve with a toss of her head and a false snigger. "At the snake?" said Adam, and went on with his reflections.

Years after Adam used to tell the whole story with the greatest humour. Eve didn't like his bringing it up. They had come up in the world since.

So does many a brave descendant of Adam today, overtaken by disaster in life, declare, "Well, thank heaven I still keep my sense of humour!" But this really shows that he hasn't got any; what he means is a brave defiance of adverse fate, which is quite another thing.

All of this in connection with the present world of war and distress and the question, referred to above, whether, as so many people express it, we can still keep our sense of humour in spite of all the disaster, the death and destruction, and worse still the outbreak of brutality and cruelty that has come over mankind. There is no danger that bravery cannot face, there is no suffering that fortitude cannot bear, but are we to think that there is no disaster that humour cannot alleviate? There are mental qualities that can be taken on at will to meet emergency, or at least increased in each of us by will – a sort of power in reserve. We can heighten our resolution, and harden our endurance, but is humour such a quality? Must we try to enlarge and stimulate our sense of humour so as to get more and more fun out of less and less material? Personally, I think not. Humour is not a weapon against war. Humour is one of the things that war can kill, that could not survive in the world if it were under the domination of force and cruelty that now lies upon Europe.

Yet here is an odd thing. All our traditional notions of war for generations back are somehow mixed up with ideas of fun and adventure, of jolly jack-tars and comic "bosuns" and a sort of rip roaring devilment that turns danger into a picnic. I say "for generations back," but let it be noted that I only mean our modern generations. The ancient world knew nothing of this attitude. The Old Testament hands out slaughter and lots of it, but it never calls it fun. It relates: "And of the Amelecks there were slain four thousand, and of the Abimilecks were slain five thousand," but it doesn't add, "but the biggest joke of all was on the Bullnecks who were *all* slain." So with the Romans and Greeks. They write calmly of putting a whole army to the sword, of passing them "under the forks," or pushing them over a cliff. That was, for them, just a plain fact – business, as it were. But neither Livy nor Tacitus would write, "One of the most amusing, indeed comic, episodes of the massacre was the drowning of Vercingetorix in his own horse-trough."

I imagine it was the age of chivalry, when knights fought on either side or both sides, at so much a throw, that turned war into a game and first opened up the idea that a battle was first-class fun.

Once started, the idea ran riot as it descended down our literature. No doubt this presentation of a gay and gallant, glorious and uproarious aspect of war helped to stimulate courage. But even at that one may doubt if it was the best sort. The courage of the Cromwellian Ironsides on their knees before battle could beat it out every time.

Yet it became, I say, a traditional attitude. Till yesterday, at least till the Great War, and that is historically yesterday, all our war memoirs and war fiction were written up with a queer false hilarity. In fact it became a convention that military episodes of death and danger must be written up as if they were one huge laugh. Take as a sample such a passage as the following, which every reader of one generation back has read a hundred times. It is taken from the book called by some such title as *Bullets, Buckshot and Bombshells*, or the *Memoirs of War Correspondents in the Karroo* – that or something else. It runs:

> I was standing between Lord Kitchener and General Roberts looking through our field glasses towards the enemy's lines which were only a hundred yards away, and laughing and joking as we always did when the enemy were about to open fire on us.
>
> Kitchener, whose wit is as keen as his sense of fun, said, "Well, why don't they start?" which threw us all into a fit of laughter. To heighten the joke he had hardly uttered the words when a veritable hail of bullets drove at us. The air seemed absolutely black with them. In fact I very seldom remember seeing the air quite so black with bullets. General Roberts, who has a deep sense of humour which sometimes comes to the surface, turned to Kitchener with a quiet smile and said, "What do you know about that?" . . . "Yes," said Kitchener, putting up his eyeglass with the greatest nonchalance, "let's go." We moved off laughing heartily. The joke was that as we went a volley of grape shot hit Kitchener in the stomach; luckily it was sideways.

One admits that that kind of writing largely passed out with the Great War. The people who used to write it have been replaced by the newer, the realistic writers who would probably transpose the episode just described, as follows:

> As the first roar of grape shot zoomed past us, my stomach suddenly sank. I walked to the edge of the mound and vomited. My stomach turned. I was sick. I threw up. "Did you vomit?" asked Lord Kitchener. I said I had. "Well, I'm going to," he said. He went and vomited. He was sick. "Did you vomit, Kitchener," said Roberts. "Yes." "Well, move aside and let me."

These newer writers, who may be described as of the "blood and guts" school, had pretty well transformed the surface of all our fiction before the present war began. They took humour out to put worse in. Later on, when in some happier day, the present war turns to history and lives again in fiction, it is not possible yet to know how it will be told. But what I am discussing here is not what will be made out of the war afterwards but what is to be made of it now. And I say, there is no humour in it.

I do not for a moment disparage the current "humour" of the London press, written in the light of incendiary fires and in the imminence of death. It's brave stuff. It is a tradition of the English people not to cry; they hate sentiment; and the Scots go even further; they keep not only their sorrow but even their jokes to themselves.

This refusal to whine, this make-believe of laughter in the face of death is grand. But there is no "humour of war" in it – nothing but resolution and pathos. And those of us far from the danger that inspires it have no right to share in it.

Indeed the more we think of it the more we realize that humour is itself one of the things at stake in this war. If the war goes wrong there will be no more humour left in the world. It will be all crushed and beaten out of it. A child will whisper to its mother, "Mother, I've thought of a joke," and will be answered, "Hush! darling, or the Gestapo will hear you." Or a bold-hearted boy might ask, "Father, who was Josh Billings?" and his father answer, "A very wicked man, my son; never speak of him."

Humour cannot share its ground with cruelty. It may be that in its earliest twilight our humour and our laughter arose out of a savage exultation over a beaten enemy. The savage cracked his enemy's head with a tomahawk, and said, "One on you!" So the theorists tell us. But that is as far back and as low as all the rest of our origin. In the world of today humour lives only with human kindliness and human freedom. It is only now when we are in danger of losing our good old democracy that we can see how fine and free it is and how individual character responds to it. Till the war came we spent our time growling at the imperfections of democracy. Democracy of course was inefficient, so it ought to be. Efficiency is an unnatural strain, like Sunday School, or company manners. Democracy was more or less crooked; so is humanity; so are you.

But democracy was everywhere permeated with humanity, and humour was the very atmosphere of its life. It presented everywhere that rare combination of humbug and sincerity which makes the world go round. It evolved the "politician" as the master genius of democracy. Chivalry evolved the knight, looking for the Holy Grail. Monarchy evolved the gentleman, hunting foxes. Democracy, in America, evolved the politician, hunting votes. This meant a man who really loved his fellows and could stand for them all day and would give everything to everybody, or promise it, and had no principles that he was not willing to sell for better ones. The politician and our democratic politics moved, if you like, in an atmosphere of humbug, of make-believe anger, and mock denunciation. A politician could boil with indignation, as easily as an egg on a heater. He would stand appalled at anything he needed to stand appalled at. The country was alternately saved or lost every two years, it moved on the brink of ruin, it rounded a corner, it emerged into the sunlight – something doing all the time. But with it all how utterly and vastly superior it has been to anything that despotism can ever offer to Europe.

Humour in Europe is dead. There hasn't been a joke in Germany for twenty-five years. Germany turns its tongue and pen to vitriolic satire, to coarse denunciation, as far from humour as blasphemy from blessing. Mussolini – it stands on record – was once an enthusiastic student of Mark Twain. He couldn't pass now.

We must keep our sense of humour till after the war. Some day we may be back again in a world of peace, in the sunshine of unprepared democracy, in the ease of inefficiency, in the out-of-door sport of politics, and humour will come into its own again.

Won't everything seem funny then? What a laugh we'll have, eh?

Memories of Christmas

Christmas Rapture

Pre-war

WELL, WELL, here's Christmas time again, and Christmas almost here! There's always a sort of excitement as it gets near, isn't there? Only this morning the postman was saying – there's a genial fellow, if you like, that postman – was saying that Christmas is right on top of us. I said, not yet, but he said, oh, yes, as good as here. He said it was real Christmas weather, too. I thought, not yet, but he insisted. He said that why he likes Christmas is that he has three kiddies, all boys. He always takes them out on Christmas. My! I hope he takes them a good long way this Christmas! Japan, eh?

The furnace man was talking too. He says I'll be having company round Christmas and so he's going to drive the furnace a bit. I tell him I don't expect much company but he says he is going to coax her along anyway. The furnace man comes from the old country and where he worked, the gentleman he worked for – this, of course, was a *real* gentleman – used to give him a goose every Christmas. Never missed. That was nice, wasn't it? The furnace man has four kiddies, all boys; he says it's a great business for him and the missus thinking what to give them all . . . I do hope they can think of something good this year.

But, as I say, as Christmas gets near there's a sort of excitement about it. Such a lot of things to go to – concerts, entertainments, all sorts of things. I don't know how I'm going to manage them all. Here's this big Police Concert, one of the first. A policeman brought tickets for it to the door yesterday – such a big, fine-looking fellow – with a revolver. I took two tickets. My, that will be a great evening, all those policemen singing together. But I don't know whether I'll go. Such a lot of police, eh? . . . But I've got the tickets upon the mantel alongside of the Firemen's Entertainment, and the Musicale for the Deaf and Dumb and a lot more. That one on the right is a new one – the *Garbage Men's Gathering*. I got that from the garbage man early this morning. My goodness! It was a piece of luck. He told me he had rung the bell twice and was just going away when I came down in my dressing-gown. Wasn't it a lucky chance! And, do you know, he says it's a new thing this Christmas, the first time the garbage men have got together. Think of it – ever since the birth of Christ.

But the bother is it's the same night as the Archaeology lecture at the university, and I mustn't miss that. Mrs. Dim – she's the wife of Professor Dim who's giving the lecture – sent me a ticket. I had sent her an azalea and she sent back the ticket right away – pretty thoughtful, eh? – and afterwards I met her on the street and she said I really must come. She said this is his *new* lecture. He's only been giving it since 1935. So there's the ticket on the mantelpiece. *The Record of the Rocks* it reads – Great title, eh? you'd wonder how a man could get a title like that. Mrs. Dim told me that Professor Dim thought and thought and thought, before he got it. I'll say he did, eh?

But of course there's one thing I certainly won't miss and that's church on Sunday morning. I'm not much of a church-goer as a rule but I never miss Christmas morning. Canon Bleet always preaches himself. He's past eighty now, but my! he's a vigorous old man! He preached an hour and a quarter last Christmas – and such a sermon. He just took the text, "Come!" – just that one word, "Come" – or, no, wait a minute, it was "Up!" . . . It was about the Hittites. He went back to Genesis, then right down to the apostles and half way back again. So I'm not going to miss that. I don't know what it's going to be this year. I hopc it'll be the Hittites again, eh?

So when you put it all together it begins to look like a pretty big day, doesn't it? And naturally the biggest part of it is Christmas Dinner! Such a dinner as I had last year at the Dobson-Dudds, a real, old-fashioned dinner, right after Church. Eat! I never ate so much in my life – turkey, plum pudding, everything. You see what makes you eat at their house is they don't have anything to drink. They are *against* it, on *principle*. Mrs. Dudd says she calls it Liberty Hall, because she lets people do just as they like. But, as she said, she's against having anything to drink because of the children seeing it. You see Mrs. Dudd was a Dobson and all the Dobsons were against it. Old Mrs. Dobson – Mrs. Dudd's mother – was there at the dinner – that was good, wasn't it? – She sat next me, and she told me they had always been against it. She told me she didn't know where the young people were getting to now; she said you go to dinner where the young girls drink cocktails and wine till it's just awful! Say – think if I'd got into a dinner like that!

But, of course, there's one good thing about not having to drink, you certainly can eat. I mean, not only turkey and that but a lot of extra things. I ate celery all the time I was waiting for the turkey. You naturally do if there's no sherry. I ate bunches of it, and afterwards a lot of parsley and part of a table wreath by mistake.

Such a dinner! We went into the drawing-room afterwards and it was great. We didn't smoke because Mrs. Dudd doesn't believe in gentlemen smoking when ladies are present. She thinks that the ladies' company ought to be enough without. So it ought, oughtn't it? However, we had a fine time looking at the photographs taken of their summer place – Liberty Cottage. I had to leave about five o'clock for Canon Dim's Happy Sunday Afternoon (he has it on Christmas, too) for the News Boys. I just made it.

Of course, naturally the great excitement before Christmas time is the question of buying presents. It takes a tremendous lot of thinking about because the real thing in giving is to think just what people would like and what would be suitable and acceptable – the kind of thing a person would like to have and keep. Often it's puzzling to know what to give. Now there's Horton. He's a stock-broker down town, and I see him often at the club, and I must give him something this year because he sent me an azalea. It was the one I sent on to Mrs. Dim. Horton has a client who is a florist, and of course that started it. Now you see I have to give a present to Horton – he's the one I say is a broker – I can't really tell what I ought to give as it all depends on the market. I had thought of giving him a Turkish rose-water Narghile pipe – but if the market all goes bad again, it might be a winter overcoat.

I said I had "thought of giving –" That's the thing, "thinking of something to give," even if in the end you don't feel quite sure and don't give it. For example, I am giving Canon Bleet an encyclopaedia. Isn't that just exactly, absolutely the thing for a scholarly clergyman? Can't you just see him starting right in at *Capital A*. and reading it all! But wait, he mustn't have it yet! You see encyclopaedias get so quickly out of date. Wait! – patience! – till the very year when there's a new one, for example, the last edition of Britannica, came out in 1927. Canon Bleet knows all that happened up to then. So I've been waiting each year to hit it right. So far no luck. But I happen to know, on the inside, that there's to be a new edition any time within ten years. That's the one for him, eh?

On the other hand some presents – I've got. I have them right here in the room – things that I wanted to make sure of. This dressing-gown (the one I have on) is for my brother George. When I got it, a little while ago, it looked a little bit too new, so I've been taking the edge off it, and of course I can't have any buttons sewn on or the ink taken out. Then here's this present for Teddy. Teddy travels a good deal, so guess what I've got him! – a travelling bag! Pretty good idea, eh? – the kind of bag you take when you travel. It's made of pig-skin. The man said so, but to look at a pig you wouldn't think it. It's too clean for a pig. I've taken a trip or two with it just to get it more like the natural pig before Teddy gets it.

And yet, somehow, I now and then think that perhaps this Christmas I'll break away a little. After all, a man ought not to get into a rut. So much church-going (every year) is apt to get a man stuck in a groove.

And the Christmas dinner stuff! The Dobson-Dudds have invited me to come again for Christmas dinner this year. But I don't think I can go. Oh, no, I mustn't. It would be imposing on them. A man mustn't always be taking the hospitality of his friends. I think this year I'll just go down and have a bite to eat at the club, with just a glass of sherry and just a bottle of red wine or a quart of Scotch whisky. Just that.

No, I'm not sure I won't alter it all. It's too exciting, too wearing – concerts, sermons, I can't keep up with it. Perhaps I'll pack up George's dressing-gown into Teddy's pigskin travelling bag and beat it out of town. Where? I don't know – perhaps I'll go up north? eh, or down south? or, say – out west, or perhaps back east, anyway, somewhere!

Christmas Shopping

Pre-war

LET ME SAY right at the start that I am devoted to Christmas – no time in the year like it. It's all brightness and light and Christmas trees with candles, and holly berries – with little children dancing in a ring and every one pretending to be a fine fellow, and pretty nearly succeeding in it.

I was brought up on it; weren't you? It was a sort of family tradition – house all hung with mottos of MERRY CHRISTMAS, and cotton wool and red flannel. . . . You had all that in your family, too, didn't you, and your brother Jim always gave your brother Dick a neck-tie every Christmas, just the same as the one Dick gave to Jim, and your mother paid for both of them – didn't she, so as to teach the children to be generous?

Quite so; and in that case you'll agree with me that of all the side issues and extras that go with Christmas and make it what it is, there isn't one that for warmth and character is in it with Christmas shopping! The pleasure of anticipation, that warm glow about the heart, eh! that joy in generous giving far ahead of getting anything for yourself. That's you, isn't it? Yes, I'm sure it is.

And, of course, as we all know, the anticipation of pleasure has in it a higher quality, in reality, than the pleasure itself. Packing a picnic lunch is better than a picnic, getting fishing tackle together is better than fishing, and looking over a travel folder called *Five Days in Sunny Jamaica* is better than living there.

So, come on out into the street in our imagination and let's go Christmas shopping!

What a picture it calls up – the clean fresh air, the streets as light as day and all full of people, the big snowflakes falling – never so big and never so slow in coming down as at Christmas time – they hate to land and miss the rest of it. . . . Snowflakes falling on the laughing crowd, on the little "tots" holding their mothers' hands, and falling on the coloured hoods and the glistening hair of the pretty girls – it takes a snowflake to pick out the prettiest. . . . All moving, swaying, laughing, talking, and going more or less nowhere!. . . Such is Christmas shopping on a winter evening.

Notice, while the picture is still before us, how all the people in the Christmas crowd of the streets are somehow lifted out of their common selves and idealized. Sour old devils of "fathers" have dropped off thirty years of age and thirty pounds of sin, every woman looks like mother, and all the girls – I swear it's not the snowflakes – have turned pretty – and the little "tots" " just mentioned – it's hard to realize how often in our home life we've called them "little pups."

Christmas shopping for me! As I sit here in my club writing about it, the thing gets hold of me. I'm going to do it this year. I've purposely left it all till this the last evening before Christmas when I am free to go at it, and as soon as I have scratched off this writing I shall go out and join the glad throng.

Christmas shopping and Christmas presents! Giving to everybody among your family and friends just the things to make them happy! Surely the thought must reach even the meanest. Doesn't it get you? Anyway, I want to have my say and give my advice about it, even if it is largely made up of "don'ts," and of warning you what not to do.

First – be very careful about the idea of starting Christmas shopping early in the year, right back in January or February, when things are being sold off. I tried that out a year or so ago. There's nothing in it. People had so often showed me things that they had "picked up" in January! Well, you know how *words* impress you and the idea of just "picking things up" makes you feel terribly superior.

People talk also of getting things "for a song," though that's mostly when they go abroad and bring back some pottery from Italy. That's too far to go for Christmas.

Anyway, I went out in January and picked up a bird-cage and a book called *The Bible Lands of Palestine* and a pair of braces (boy's size). I admit the things were cheap. The bird-cage was only thirty cents, and it was worth thirty dollars. The man in the shop admitted this himself, but it's been no good to me. I know no one with a bird. People don't seem to keep birds now. Yet this is a fine cage, big enough for a penguin, with a bar for it to swing on and little places where you put in food and water, and other little places where you take out whatever you take out. Too bad, I can't use it; I may offer it in a raffle for a charity . . . however, let it go.

The Bible Lands of Palestine was a beautiful-looking book, fine binding and lovely illustrations – one of some one bathing, not naked, of course, in a lovely flat river with lovely sand beside it and lovely little sheep or lambs nibbling the daintiest of grass – you know how pink and yellow and dainty Palestine is. There was another picture of men in a boat on a lake, with tossing waves; in fact it's getting pretty rough. I couldn't quite make out the idea. It might have been a dinghy race, only the boat looked too round and slow. Perhaps they were just out for a sail. . . . All I mean is that it was a lovely book and I was just wrapping it up to give away when I saw on the front blank page, very dim, but still readable, the inscription, *The Reverend*

James Peabody from his Mother. . . . I started to rub it out and had got it pretty well off, but I went on rubbing too far and saw another inscription, *The Reverend John Somebody from his Mother* . . . and underneath that another, *The Reverend Thomas Something from his Mother*. I thought of cutting the page out, but it was no good as there were more half-rubbed-out inscriptions on the next one, to more clergymen from their mothers; and beyond that there seemed to be, still more dim, inscriptions that ended . . . "from her affectionate son." So they must have passed the book round both ways. . . . Of course, I still have the book and have the pleasure of looking at the pictures – that one I mentioned of the dinghy in rough weather and another of a man carrying a huge bed on his back – for a bet, evidently. . . . But it's no good for Christmas.

The other item was the braces – twenty-five cents and worth two dollars, suitable for a boy of fourteen, but with a little wheel to jack them up to a boy of sixteen. Boys grow so fast; all mothers and fathers will get the idea of that little wheel. But I want to speak about these twenty-five-cent braces, and I want to speak seriously and especially to mothers and fathers. That's no present to give to a boy, and you know it! You don't understand me? Oh, yes, you do. You've no right to give a boy something *useful* – something he's got to have. To give a boy for Christmas a pair of braces, or six collars, or an overcoat, or a pair of winter gloves, or anything that's useful and that he has to have and that you've got to buy for him sooner or later, is just a low-down-trick unworthy of the spirit of Christmas.

With little girls, of course, it's quite different. They're easy. You see, the little pups love finery, and you can give them ribbons, laces, shoes – anything. They're just inexhaustible. But when a boy thinks of Christmas he knows just what he wants. I mean, not the particular thing, but the kind of properties and qualities that it's got to have. It has to be something more or less mechanical, more or less mysterious, with either wheels in it or electricity, a something that "goes" – you know what I mean. Well, next time you want to buy a Christmas present for a little boy, you go to the toy department of any big store and say to the man – now remember, not to a woman, she can't understand – "I want to buy for a little boy something that goes when you start it, has mechanism and an element of the mysterious, either cogged wheels or a battery. . . ." And he'll say, "Exactly!" and lead you right to it. There it is, take it out of its box – boys' presents have to be big – it's marked *COGGO! The New Mechanico-Thermic Wonder!* . . . Can't you see the fascination of it?

That reminds me – you don't mind my telling a story in the middle of an article; I'm just writing as I go – years and years ago I got one of those things to give to my little son at Christmas. It was sent up to the house that evening when the child was asleep. But three (middle-aged) professors were dining with me, when the big parcel with *COGGO* was handed in, and one, a professor of mediaeval history, said, "Let's look at it." Then another, professor of Roman Law, said, "How does it go?" and the third, a professor of mechanics, said, "I think this way." So I said, "Wait a minute, we'll clear the table." But they said, "No, put it on the floor – more space." We had a fine time with it, till we broke it.

So you see – I'm speaking here to fathers only – if you do buy the boy one of these big mechanical toys remember that even if they are expensive you *yourself* can have a lot of fun with them. That ought to count, eh? And not only yourself. Ask in your clergyman and any J.P. or general or Member of Parliament that you know. They'll enjoy it. . . .

But I repeat – don't buy the useful things. Those braces – I never gave them away. I have them still. As I stood with them in my hand thinking where to send them, my mind conjured up a picture of how I felt, long ago, over sixty years ago, when I opened my stocking one Christmas and found, all wrapped up in boxes and parcels that might have been filled with magic, just such junk as that. There was a little round hard box with a tight lid that might have opened out to be magic music, or goodness knows what – for a child's imagination outstrips reality – but it was only collars. I had hard work to choke back tears. And after that – flat and long and mysterious – was a box that might have held – why, anything! Derringer pistols, Cherokee daggers, anything. . . . But did it? No. It had in it a pair of braces just like these, wheel and all. That broke me down. . . . There is no blame; all parents do it, must do it, in such a crowded family as ours was, with a census that went up each year. But at least let me plead for some one present, however trivial, with the true touch in it of the magic of the mysterious. . . . My own case I wrote up and wrote off long ago, as a story, *Hoodoo McFiggin's Christmas*, in my book, *Literary Lapses*, where it stands as a warning.

Did I give those braces away? No, sir. Give them to some poor child? No, sir, there is no child so poor that I should wish that evil gift upon him. I wear those braces myself, wheel and all between my shoulder blades, as a monk wears a hair shirt, to remind me of the true spirit of Christmas. . . .

But, *per contra*, in the other direction, never make the mistake of asking a boy – I mean a little, little boy, too young for discretion – of asking him what he'd want for Christmas. If you do, he'll say right off, no hesitation: a horse, and a baby motor car, and a big radio, like grandmammas's. Then, where are you? But come back again to the street. Let's go shopping.

And here we reach the question of buying Christmas presents at any time through the year, just when you happen to see anything that looks nice for somebody. It is a good plan, only don't you find – I speak just as between you and me – that the things you see, or at least that attract your attention, are the ones that are just right for yourself? You see in a shop window a pipe, a beautiful thing in a case, and you say to yourself, "The very thing for a Christmas present." Your conscience says, "Present for whom?" But you stifle it. At first you try to call it "Charlie's pipe," meaning it for your brother. But, well, Charlie never sees it. It's gone the way of George's fishing-rod, the nickel-plated cigar-lighter your nephew never saw. Still, it's all right. You can make it up to them later. You can do as I am doing tonight the moment I finish this writing, just go out and have one big grand unselfish burst of present buying, among all the little tots and the laughing crowds I spoke of. Something for everybody this time! No one forgotten. I think I'll write them down on a list – you've tried it, haven't you; George and Mary (something for their house, they haven't been married long); Charlie, a pipe; my great-niece Nancy (three and a half; you ought to see her), either a pearl necklace, or, no, I'll see when I get there. . . .

And this time there must be no hesitation, no doubt. That's fatal to Christmas shopping. I look back over bygone years and I think of all the presents I meant to give but didn't. No doubt, as you'll say at once, I'm all the better man for meaning to give them. I admit it. But I think in that respect I don't need to get any better still.

Everybody, I am sure, has had the same experience of presents never given. There was a man many many years ago who did me a great kindness. He took my classes when I was a schoolmaster and enabled me to get off for three weeks to write on college examinations. When I went to pay him he wouldn't take anything. It meant a lot to me, both ways. But I didn't thank him over effusively or show too much emotion. I meant that actions should speak louder than words. I decided to give him a watch at Christmas. Then I went a little further and decided on a gold watch, the kind of watch he would never buy for himself, for he was not well off – one to last all his life. The watch being gold, I couldn't give it to him that Christmas; but what's a year, or what was it then? His watch was coming and it gave me pleasure, whenever I met him, to think that once given he had his watch for life. So he would have had – but he didn't. The Christmases went by; the time never came when I could quite, or not without – well, you understand. I never gave it to him. And now I never can; where he is, he's too happy to need it.

But it was a kind thought, anyway. I've had quite a few like that. There is a man going round in Montreal wearing, for me, though he doesn't know it, a smoking jacket that I nearly gave him the Christmas after he got married. There is, or was, a retired clergyman who nearly qualified for an encyclopaedia; and ever so many of my young married friends have imaginary sets of Shakespeare. But I needn't explain it. I am sure that you yourself, and everybody else, have a list of these gifts that never were given. It is very sweet of you to have thought of them. Perhaps this Christmas you might make good on one or two. Change the encyclopaedia to a fountain-pen or, if you like, to a pencil sharpener; only give it, don't wait. But it is getting late – the shops will close soon. . . .

I append this note to what I wrote above. Too bad. Another Christmas gone wrong. I had no idea that the crowds were as thick as that, and as noisy. And the children – the ones I called tots – I don't think people ought to be allowed to bring out children in such bunches as that! And those things the little devils blow into! That's against the law. The noise, all yelling at once and laughing! What is there to laugh about? Get into the shops – you can't! They're jammed to the doorway. Why can't they let a man with a list just walk in and pick out what he wants and go home? No place for him. I didn't even try to get through the crowds; in fact, I didn't get more than fifty feet round the main street corner.

Now that I'm back in the club I'll have to do the best I can about presents. I have, right here in the club, a bottle of Scotch whisky for George and Mary – John, the hall porter, suggested it; he's from Scotland. At any rate, I have the bottle all wrapped up to take home with me, and the bird-cage I spoke of, I'll find some one for that. Later, Charlie can have *The Bible Lands of Palestine*, and for little Nancy – either a bottle of port or two hundred cigarettes.

I've spoiled another Christmas by too much planning and romancing, a mistake we all make, loading it up with sentiment instead of getting down to facts. Next year, I'll know better.

Yes, John, put the port under my other arm and the cigarettes in my overcoat pocket. Good night. . . . Merry Christmas!

War-time Santa Claus

I ONCE ASKED a Christmas Eve group of children if they believed in Santa Claus. The very smallest ones answered without hesitation, "Why, of course!" The older ones shook their heads. The little girls smiled sadly but said nothing. One future scientist asserted boldly, "I know who it is"; and a little make-strong with his eye on gain said: "I believe in it all; I can believe anything." That boy, I realized, would one day be a bishop.

Thus does the bright illusion of Santa Claus fade away. The strange thing is that it could ever exist. It shows how different from ours are children's minds, as yet unformed and nebulous and all unbounded, still bright with the glory of the infinite. As yet physical science, calling itself the truth, has not overclouded them. There is no reason for them why a bean should not grow into a bean-stalk that reaches the sky in one night; no reason why a dog should not have eyes as big as the round tower of Copenhagen; no reason why a white cat should not, at one brave stroke of a sword, turn into a princess. Are not all these things known by children to be in books, read aloud to them in the firelight just when their heads begin to nod toward bedtime and the land of dreams more wonderful still?

We have to realize that the child's world is without economic purpose. A child doesn't understand – happy ignorance – that people are paid to do things. To a child the policeman rules the street for self-important majesty; the furnace man stokes the furnace because he loves the noise of falling coal and the fun of getting dirty; the grocer is held to his counter by the lure of aromatic spices and the joy of giving. And in this very ignorance there is a grain of truth. The child's economic world may be the one that we are reaching out in vain to find. Here is a bypath in the wood of economics that some day might be followed to new discovery. Meantime, the children know it well and gather beside it their flowers of beautiful illusion.

This Land of Enchantment of the child – with its Santa Claus and its Magic Grocer – breaks and dissolves slowly. But it has to break. There comes a time when children suspect, and then when they know, that Santa Claus is Father. Worse still, there comes a time when they get to know that Father, so to speak, is not Santa Claus – no longer the all-wonderful, all-powerful being that drew them on a little sleigh, and knew everything and told them about it. Father seems different when children realize that the geography-class teacher knows more than he does, and that Father sometimes drinks a little too much, and quarrels with Mother. Pity we can't keep their world of illusion a little longer from shattering. It's not Santa Claus only that fades out. It's ourselves.

Then at last there comes to children the bitter fruit from the tree of economic knowledge. This shows them that the furnace man works for money, and that the postman doesn't carry letters just for the fun of giving them in at the door. If it were not that new ideas and interests come to children even in this dilapidation, their disillusionment might pass into an old age, broken-hearted for ever at its farewell to giants and fairies. One thinks of the overwise child of Gilbert's *Bab Ballads*: "Too precocious to thrive, he could not keep alive, and died an enfeebled old dotard at five."

Yet even after disillusionment, belief lingers. Belief is a survival instinct. We have to have it. Children growing older, and their mothers growing younger by living with them, cling to Santa Claus. If he is really not so, he has to be brought back again as a symbol, along with the Garden of Eden and Noah's Ark. No longer possible as a ruddy and rubicund old man with a snow-white corona of whiskers, he lives again as a sort of spirit of kindliness that rules the world, or at least once a year breaks into any house to show it what it might be.

But does he? Is there such a spirit in our world? Can we believe in Santa Claus?

All through life we carry this wondering question, these tattered beliefs, these fading visions seen through a crystal that grows dim. Yet, strangely enough, often at their dimmest, some passing breath of emergency, of life or death and sacrifice of self, clears the glass of the crystal and the vision is all there again. Thus does life present to all of us its alternations of faith and doubt, optimism and pessimism, belief and negation.

Is the world a good place or a bad? An accident or a purpose? Down through the ages in all our literatures echoes the cry of denunciation against the world. *Sunt lachrymae rerum*, mourned the Roman poet – the world is full of weeping; and Shakespeare added, "All our yesterdays have lighted fools the way to dusty death." Yet the greatest denunciation is not in the voice of those who cry most loudly. Strutting Hamlet in his velvet suit calls out, "The time is out of joint," and egotism echoes it on. But far more poignant is the impotent despair of those whose life has wearied to its end, disillusioned, and who die turning their faces to the wall, still silent.

Is that the whole truth of it? Can life really be like that? With no Santa Claus in it, no element of mystery and wonder, no righteousness to it? It can't be. I remember a perplexed curate of the Church of England telling me that he felt that "after all, there must be a kind of something." That's just exactly how I feel about it. There must be something to believe in, life must have its Santa Claus.

What's more, we never needed Santa Claus so badly as we do at this present Christmas. I'm going to hang up my stocking anyway. Put yours there beside it. And I am going to write down the things I want Santa Claus to bring, and pin it up beside the stocking. So are you? Well, you wait till I've written mine first! Can't you learn to be unselfish at Christmas time?

So, first I'll tell Santa Claus that I don't want any new presents, only just to have back some of the old ones that are broken – well, yes, perhaps I broke them myself. Give me back, will you, that pretty little framed certificate called Belief in Humanity; you remember – you gave them to ever so many of us as children to hang up beside our beds. Later on I took mine out to look what was on the back of it, and I couldn't get it back in the frame and lost it.

Well, I'd like that and – oh, can I have a new League of Nations? You know, all set up on a rack that opens in and out. I broke the old one because I didn't know how to work it, but I'd like to try again. And may I have a brand new Magna Carta, and a Declaration of Independence and a Rights of Man and a Sermon on the Mount? And I'd like, if you don't mind, though of course it's more in the way of a toy, a little Jack-in-the-Box, one with a little Adolf Hitler in it. No, honestly, I wouldn't hurt him; I'd just hook the lid and keep him for a curiosity. I can't have it? Never mind.

Here, listen, this is what I want, Santa Claus, and here I'm speaking for all of us, millions and millions of us.

Bring us back the World We Had, and didn't value at its worth – the Universal Peace, the Good Will Towards Men – all that we had and couldn't use and broke and threw away.

Give us that. This time we'll really try.

War-time Christmas

AFTER ALL – it's Christmas. It may seem to us the most distressed, the most tragic Christmas of the ages – Christmas in a world of disaster never known before. But yet, it's Christmas. And we ought to keep it so as the old, glad season of goodwill towards man, and kindliness and forgiveness towards everybody. Notice, towards everybody – even towards Adolf Hitler. What? You say you'd rather boil him in oil. Oh, but, of course, I *include* that; boil him, and then forgive him boiled. So with all the Germans – I'd like to drown them all in the Rhine, and then forgive then and send the Rhine to the wash.

A tragic Christmas – and yet, I don't know. When I begin to think of it, I am not sure whether it *is* tragic. It is a Christmas of disaster, but what is that? That passes away and is gone. But for the things that do not pass away, the permanent forces in human life, perhaps this Christmas is to be for us the most ennobling, the most inspiring of all there have been since the first Christmas announced salvation to the world.

I am thinking here of what has been done in England – the steady heroism of a whole nation that has gone out as a new light to lighten the world. This inspiration from England may prove, and I think it will, the first guidance towards a new world.

And when I say England, I must at once explain that I include Scotland and Wales and Northern Ireland and, naturally, the Isle of Man. People are so touchy on this point, especially since the war began, that I should not wish to hurt any one's feelings. When I say England and an Englishman, to me every Manxman is an Englishman, and every Welshman a Scotchman, and both Englishmen. For what else can you say? You can't say "a British"; that's not sense; nor a "Briton" because that means an Ancient Briton, stained blue, and studying with an axe to be a qualified Druid. Let him stay in the mistletoe; we don't want him.

So in the sense I mean, we can say that the word "Englishman" has taken on for the world a new meaning. Some people saw it long ago. W.S. Gilbert, of Gilbert and Sullivan, showed it to us fifty years back in his immortal verse:

> For he might have been a Russian,
> A Turk or else a Prussian,
> Or an Ital-ey-an.
> But in spite of all temptation
> To belong to another nation,
> He was born an Englishman.

People thought at the time that this was meant to be funny, and laughed at it. But we see now that Gilbert was just stating the quiet truth and was laughed at for it, as humourists always are.

"He was born an Englishman?" . . . Who wouldn't be? And all the world is being reborn into that heritage – which is the real, the spiritual meaning of this Christmas.

For me, I must have it so. For I cannot let Christmas go. Christmas has always seemed to me a day of enchantment, and the world about us on Christmas day, for one brief hour an enchanted world. On Christmas morning the streets are always bright with snow, not too much of it nor too little, hard-frozen snow, all crystals and glittering in the flood of sunshine that goes with Christmas day. . . . If there was ever any other Christmas weather I have forgotten it. . . . Only the memory of the good remains.

Into this enchanted world I step on Christmas morning, to walk the street and meet and greet at once, it seems, an enchanted friend. God bless the fellow! How happy and rosy and friendly he looks, and he draws off his glove to shake my hand – rosy and handsome in his silk hat (why doesn't he wear it every day?) and his white neckerchief. . . . He must be sixty if he's a day, but on Christmas morning he looks a boy again, and he and I are back at school together. I must see more of him; true, I saw him at the club yesterday but he didn't look like this; something grouchy about him, taciturn sort of fellow – but on Christmas morning I can see him as he really is. . . . But I no sooner leave him than I seem to run into half a dozen like him; the street seems full of them, all silk hats and white neckcloths . . . and "Merry Christmas!" here and "Merry Christmas!" there . . . old boys hauling sleighs with little granddaughters done up in furs . . . or with a little convoy of great-nieces and grand-nephews. "Merry Christmas, children." Upon my word, I hadn't realized what a pleasant lot of friends I had.

No doubt you feel the same enchantment as I do! And it follows you all through Christmas day – at the dinner with the enchanted turkey, with every one a good fellow, and every good fellow wearing a tissue paper hat . . . the dinner followed by an enchanted sleigh-ride . . . with old friends, and meeting new people as you go – and every one of them so delightful . . . the world so generous, so bright. And then somehow the brightness passes, the light fades out, and it is tomorrow. You are back in the dull world of every day – anxious, suspicious, every man for himself. Friends? Which of them would lend me fifty dollars – come, I'll make it five!

This enchanted Christmas always seems to me to be a part of that super-self, that higher self that is in each of us, but that only comes to the surface in moments of trial or exaltation and in the hour of death. The super-self is always within call, and yet we cannot call it. I don't mean here the thing called the subconscious self, that evil, inward thing that can take my sleeping hand and write upon a slate, that can tell me where I lost my umbrella, or through a psycho-analyst betray by my dreams that for years I have had a complex to murder my aunt.... Not that hideous stuff; nor any of the "complexes" and "behaviours" and "reactions," the new hideous brood of the new Black Art. Oh, no, I mean something infinitely more open, more above-board, more radiant than that ... that light that shines in people's eyes who clasp hands and face danger together ... the surge of sacrifice within the heart that lifts the individual life above itself.

All lovers – silly lovers in their silly stage – attain for a moment this super-self, each as towards the other. Each sees in the other what would be there for all the world to see in each of us, if we could but reach to it. "She thinks he's wonderful," says her mocking friends. "He thinks she's a lulu!" laugh his associates. She *is* a lulu, and he *is* wonderful – till the light passes and is gone. "All the world loves a lover" – of course; one can see easily why.

It is towards this higher self – not as momentary exaltation but as sustained endeavour – that this Christmas of disaster is calling us. "Come up!" it beckons. "You must. There is no other way. This is the salvation of the world – come!"... And on the answer is staked all the future of mankind.

For this altered world is not like anything that went before. Think back, as all people even in middle life can do, to what the world was like while the World War was just a dream, the vague theme of a romance.

To realize this alteration, come back with me in recollection, to church together – to an evening service, on Christmas Eve.... Quiet and dim the church seems, the lights low, and from the altar comes the voice, half reading, half intoned, and from the dimness of the body of thc church the murmur of the responses . . . *Give peace in our time, O Lord* . . . Peace! Why, it was always peace! What did we know then of world war, of world brutality, of the concentration camp and the mass-slaughter of the innocent?

The responses echo back . . . *because there is none other that fighteth for us but only Thou, O Lord* . . . but what meaning could the words convey? nothing, or little – just a compliment murmured in the dark. . . . *Strengthen her that she may vanquish and overcome all her enemies* . . . yes, but what enemies had she? Only a few poor Matabeles and Afridis, and such . . . Vanquish them? Yes, of course, but then teach them to play cricket and mix a gin-fizz, and be part of the British Empire and ride in a barouche at a Jubilee, and then go out and help us conquer more. . . .

From plague and pestilence and famine . . . The voice is intoning the litany now, the prayer for deliverance . . . *from plague and pestilence and famine, from battle and murder and from sudden death* . . . and the murmured response through the church . . . *Good Lord, deliver us*. . . . The words are old, far older than the rubric of the church that uses them, handed down from prayer to prayer, since the days of the Barbarian Conquests of Europe, when they first went up as a cry of distress, a supplication. . . . But can the ear not catch, in this new hour, the full meaning that was here – the cry of anguish that first inspired the prayer . . . *to show thy mercy upon all prisoners and captives*. . . . In this, too, is now an infinity of meaning, of sympathy, of suffering . . . and as the service draws to its close: *While there is time* . . . intones the voice from the half darkness, *while there is time* . . . What? What is that he is saying – *while there is time?* . . . Does it mean it may be too late. . . .

Not if we can listen each of us to the call, the inspiration of this darkened Christmas . . . the call of our higher selves. Up! Up! We have no other choice. We've got to.

Goodwill Stuff

Cricket for Americans

AT THE PRESENT hour all of us who are British are anxious to cultivate cordial relations with the United States. It has occurred to me that something could be done here with cricket. Americans, I fear, do not understand our national British game, and lack sympathy with it. I remember a few years ago attending a county match in England with an American friend, and I said to him at noon on Wednesday (the match had begun on Monday), "I'm afraid that if it keeps on raining they'll have to draw stumps." "Draw what?" he said. "Draw out the wickets," I answered, "and call the game ended." "Thank God," he answered. Yet this was a really big game, a county match – Notts against Hants, I think, but perhaps Bucks against Yorks. Anyway it was a tense, exciting game, Notts (or Bucks) with 600 runs leading by 350, four wickets down, and only another six hours to play.

Ever since that day I meant to try to put the game in a better light, and then people in America could understand how wonderful it is.

Perhaps I should explain that, all modesty apart, when I speak of cricket I speak of what I know. I played cricket for years and years. I still have a bat. Once, as I mentioned in an earlier section of this book, I played in an All-Canada match at Ottawa before the Governor-General. I went in first in the first innings, and was bowled out by the first ball; but in the second innings I went in last, and by "playing back" quickly on the first ball I knocked down the wickets before the ball could reach them. Lord Minto told me afterwards that he had never seen batting like mine before, except perhaps in India, where the natives are notoriously quick.

Let me begin with a few simple explanations. Cricket is played with eleven on a side, provided you can get eleven. It isn't always easy to get a cricket team and sometimes you have to be content with ten or nine or even less. This difficulty of getting men for a side really arises from the fact that cricketers are not paid to play. They wouldn't take it, or rather they do take it when they can get it, but then they are professionals. This makes a distinction in English cricket as between players and gentlemen, although, as a matter of fact, a great many gentlemen are first-class players, and nowadays, at any rate, a good many of the players are gentlemen, and, contrawise, quite a number of the gentlemen are not quite what you would call gentlemen. I'm afraid I haven't brought out the distinction very clearly. Perhaps I may add that when we play cricket in Canada there is no question of gentlemen.

So, as I say, although cricket is properly played with eleven on a side, it is often difficult to get enough. You have to be content with what you can bring, and pick up one or two others when you get there. When I played in the All-Canada game at Ottawa, we had nine at the start, but we got one more in the hotel and one in the barbershop. When the All-England team goes to Australia they easily get eleven men, because that is different. That's twelve thousand miles. But when it's only from one town to the next it's hard to get more than seven or eight.

But let me explain the game. Cricket is played by bowling a ball up and down a "pitch" of 22 yards (roughly 66 feet, approximately) at each end of which are set three upright sticks called wickets. A batsman stands just in front of each set of wickets, a little at the side, and with his bat stops the ball from hitting the wickets. If the ball hits the wickets he is out, but otherwise not. Thus if he begins on

Monday and his wickets are not hit on Monday he begins again on Tuesday; and so on; play stops all Sunday.

Of course, when you are looking on at a cricket match, you are not supposed to shout and yell the way we do over baseball on our side of the water in Canada and in the States. All you do is to say every now and then, "Oh, very pretty, sir, very pretty!" You are speaking to the batsman, who is about two hundred yards away and can't hear you. But that doesn't matter; you keep right on: "Oh, well done, sir, well done."... That day of the county match in England that I spoke of, my American friend heard an Englishman on the other side of him say, "Oh, very pretty! Very pretty, sir," and he asked the Englishman what was very pretty. But of course the Englishman had no way of telling him. He didn't know him. So my friend turned to me and asked, "What did he do?" And I explained that it wasn't what he did, it was what he didn't do.

A great many things in good cricket turn on that – what you don't do. You let the ball go past you, for instance, instead of hitting it, and the experts say, "Oh, well let alone, sir." There are lots more balls coming; you've three days to wait for one. In the game of which I speak, the really superb piece of play was this: the bowler sent a fast ball through the air right straight towards the batsman's face; he moved his face aside and let it pass, and they called, "Well let alone, sir." You see, if it had hit him on the side of his face, he'd have been out. How out? Why, by what is called L.B.W. I forget what the letters exactly stand for, but we use them just as in the States you use things like P.W.A., A.A.C., and S.S.E. and R.I.P. You know what they are about, though you can't remember what they stand for. Well, L.B.W. is a way of getting out in cricket. It means that if you stand in front of the ball and it hits you – not your bat, but you – you are out. Suppose, for instance, you deliberately turn your back on the ball and it rises up and hits you right behind in the middle of your body – out! L.B.W.

There was a terrible row over this a few years ago in connection with one of the great Test Matches between

England and Australia. These, of course, are the great events, the big things every year in the cricket world. An All-England team goes out once a year to play Test Matches in Australia, and an All-Australian team comes to England once a year for Test Matches. As soon as they know which is really best, they can have a real match. Meantime they keep testing it out. Well, a few years ago the Australians started the idea of bowling the ball terribly fast, and right straight at the batsman, not at the wickets, so as to hit him on purpose. Even if he started to run away from the wickets they'd get him, even if he was halfway to the home tent. I didn't see it myself, but I understand that was the idea of it. So there was a tremendous row about it, and bad feeling, with talk of Australia leaving the British Empire. However, outsiders intervened and it was suggested (the Archbishop of Canterbury, I think) that the rule should be that if the bowler meant to hit the man to put him out, then he wasn't out, but that if he didn't mean to hit and he hit him, then he was out. Naturally the bowler had to be put on his honour whether he meant it. But that didn't bother the Australians; they were willing to go on their honour. They're used to it. In fact the English agreed too, that when they got the ball in their turn they'd go on their honour in throwing it at an Australian.

That, of course, is the nice thing about cricket – the spirit of it, the sense of honour. When we talk of cricket we always say that such a thing "isn't cricket," meaning that it's not a thing you would do. You could, of course. There'd be nothing to stop you, except that, you see, you couldn't. At a cricket game, for example, you never steal any of the other fellows' things out of the marquee tent where you come and go. You ask why not? Well, simply that it "isn't cricket." Or take an example in the field and you'll understand it better. Let me quote with a little more detail the case to which I referred earlier in the book. We'll say that you're fielding at "square leg." That means that you are fielding straight behind the batter's back and only about twenty-five feet away from him. Well, suppose you happen to be day-dreaming a little – cricket is a dreamy game – and the batter happens to swing round hard on a passing ball and pastes it right into the middle of your stomach. As soon as you are able to speak you are supposed to call to the bowler, "Awfully sorry, old man;" not sorry you got hit in the stomach, sorry you missed the chance he gave you; because from the bowler's point of view you had a great opportunity, when you got hit in the stomach, of holding the ball against your stomach – which puts the batter out.

So you see when you play cricket there comes in all the time this delicate idea of the cricket spirit. A good deal of English government is carried on this way. You remember a few years ago the case of a very popular Prime Minister who used to come to the House – that means the House of Commons – and say, "I'm afraid, gentlemen, I've made another mess again with this business of Italy and Ethiopia; damned if I can keep track of them; that's the third mess I've made this year." And the House wouldn't vote him out of office. It wouldn't have been cricket. Instead, they went wild with applause because the Prime Minister had shown the true cricket spirit by acknowledging that he was beaten, though of course he didn't know when he had been licked. And, for the matter of that, he'd come all the way down from Scotland just for the purpose at the very height of the grouse season – or the fly season – anyway, one of those insect seasons that keep starting in Scotland when the heather is bright with the gillies all out full.

Looking back over what I have written above, I am afraid I may have given a wrong impression here and there. When I implied that the two batsmen stand at the wicket and stop the ball, I forgot to say that every now and then they get impatient, or indignant, and not only stop it but hit it. And do they hit it! A cricket ball is half as heavy again as a baseball and travels farther. I've seen Don Bradman, the Australian, playing on our McGill University grounds, knock the ball clean over the stadium and then over the tops of the trees on the side of Mount Royal, and from there on. They had to stop the game and drink shandygaff while they sent a boy to get the ball. They almost thought of getting a new one.

And when I talked of hitting a cricketer in the stomach with the ball I forgot to explain how awfully difficult it is to do it. Not that they've no stomach – no, indeed, plenty! – you don't train *down* for cricket, you fill *up*. But the point is that the cricketer will catch any kind of ball before you can hit him. And can they catch! You'll see a fellow playing cover-point – that's northeast half a point east from the bat, distance twenty yards – and a ball is driven hard and fast above his head, and he'll leap in the air with one hand up, and, *while still in the air*, leap up a little farther still, and smack! goes the ball into his one hand. Can you wonder that the spectators all murmur, "Oh, very pretty, sir"?

And in point of excitement you think cricket slow, but can't you see how the excitement slowly gathers and all piles up at the end? Two totals coming closer and closer together – fifty to tie, fifty-one to win, twenty to tie, twenty-one to win – then three to tie, four to win – one smashing hit will do it now! Ah, there she goes! – high above the pavilion, a boundary hit for four! "Oh, very nice, sir, very nice!"

Oh, yes, cricket's all right. Let's have a shandygaff.

Our American Visitors

As Seen from Canada

NO, IT'S NOT just a matter of money, although of course we're always glad to get it, and the more you bring of it the better. . . . But that's not the real point. Let me explain it. Did you ever meet an innkeeper, one of the real old-fashioned type, dating down from the days of the stage-coach? You have, eh? Well, what is his animating motive? Money? No – Hospitality – genuine, open-hearted hospitality. He really thinks that all these people are *staying* with him, as his guests – that's how the word got into the trade – they're his *Guests*, see, staying in his house, and he's trying to make them comfortable . . . no trouble is too great.

In fact, a real hotel man can get into a sort of permanent mental delusion on this point. Such a one I recall in particular as exceeding even his own class. His fixed impression, irremovable after years of habit, was that his "guests" had come into town to pay him a personal visit; they might, of course, have a little business on the side, but the main idea was that of a friendly renewal of acquaintance. He would say to me: "We had your brother and his wife with us for a few days last week. We're always so delighted when they come – I wanted them to stay for the week end but they couldn't." . . . His hotel, and no wonder, was always full; indeed, he loved to have to give up his own sitting room, then his bedroom – sleep in a cupboard, anything – at the call of hospitality.

Well, that's how we feel about the coming of our American visitors in Canada. They're our "guests." We have the delusion that we've invited them up and that nothing is too good for them. I admit to the feeling myself; my impression is that I am entertaining, personally, about fifty thousand a week. I insist that they must see the Laurentians. I can't let them go without having them go down the St. Lawrence and see the old-fashioned French country of the Island of Orleans, and, of course, up the St. Lawrence to Lake Huron, and sideways from the St. Lawrence and then edgeways from it. I insist on their seeing a lot of things that I have never seen myself. I wave my arm round a thousand miles of scenery and give it to them.

And of course the Americans reciprocate. If I tell them they simply must see the Georgian Bay, they say they certainly will. I tell them that it has thirty-three thousand islands, and they say, "Think of that!"... "Mother," says the man at the driving wheel, "I guess we won't miss that," and they're off for it. Last year I sent some to the Great Bear Lake. I forgot the distance. I don't think they're back yet.

Now I'll tell you what I think is the main idea at the back of all this – this coming and going, this pleasure in giving away and receiving scenery, this pleasant make-believe of host and guest. It's that old-fashioned urge called peace on earth, goodwill toward men. The more it is darkened over in Europe, the more brightly does it shine with us. This solid unity of North America, put behind the heroic cause of Britain, is what is saving the world, visibly already saving it. But you could never get it by mere treaties and agreements and such; not even common interest would bring it, or not in its most real shape. It has to depend on personal feeling, on mutual acquaintance, on seeing and knowing one another.

Come on up. I'll show you the Island of Orleans – I'll show you Niagara Falls, or no, I forget, half of it is yours; I won't show it; it's not so much anyway; we just keep it for

English visitors. But I'll show the new mining district round Noranda, and I'll take you to the wild country along the Algoma Central – that is, if you fish. You do? You're crazy over it? Well, say, get right into your car and come on up. I'll have the bait ready.

A Welcome to a Visiting American

At the Canadian National Exhibition

WELL NOW! That's fine to see you! I felt sure I'd run into American friends here at the Canadian National Exhibition. I've been writing so much in the papers to invite them up that I felt sure I'd find some of them here. When did you come up? Just here, eh? And got a fortnight for a trip to Canada? That's good. Let me take you round and I can tell you about everything here and talk about your trip.

You don't want to listen to the speeches in the Grand Stand, do you? No, of course not, You get them at home. Of course you must have a Fall Fair much like this in your state at home, I suppose – you do, eh? – with farm machinery and prize hogs – same as we have, eh? – and a Midway with a troupe of Syrian Dancing Girls from the Palmyra desert – think of those same girls getting all the way out to you!

No, I haven't seen the machinery yet, nor the hogs, have you? I meant to, in fact I have been meaning to for some forty-odd years. So it's the same with you, eh?

You ask, what was that song they sang at the opening – that's *God Save the King*. You thought it was *Sweet Land of Liberty*? So it is. You Yankees took it from us and put new words to it. As a matter of fact we took it from the Ancient Britons – they had it, *England-may-go-to-Hell* –

and the English liked it so much they took it over and made it *God Save the King*.

Hard to get new music, isn't it? Unless you're a Dago. Of course we have a fine song up here, *O Canada*, but most of us don't know the words, and those that do don't know the music, and most people don't know both, so the song generally fades away after a line or so. Then there's another, *The Maple Leaf*. You may have heard it. It runs – "The Maple Leaf, The Maple Leaf, for ever," and it goes on like that for ever.

But *God Save the King* is the best. It's so darned patriotic, and it's easy. Once you get it going you can fairly shout it . . . "Send him vic-to-rious, hap-pee and glo-rious," eh, what? . . . The only bother is it's hard to start. At the close of our meetings the chairman always says, "Will some one please start *God Save the King*." There's a long silence. Then some man hidden in the audience starts, away down in his throat, "G-o-d!" He gets no takers. Another one a little way off and a little higher, begins "G-o-d . . ." then two or three more, "G-o-d," till all of a sudden, you never know how, out they come, "God save our –" and they're off.

So you're going to take a drive into the North Country? Yes, I certainly recommend that – wonderful wild country, all lakes and islands, and, of course, the new mining district. The Dionne Quintuplets? Yes, you pass them on the way, at Callander, so I suppose it's worth while. But personally I think they've been greatly exaggerated. There are still only five of them.

But the North Country – now that is worth while. And I'll give you a piece of good advice. Take your fishing tackle along with you. Whatever people go up there for, it always turns sooner or later into fishing. I saw a university professor going up last week to make a report to the government on Indian dialects. Say, you ought to have seen the trout he brought back. . . . Not one under three pounds; and he said he'd been sending them out by express for days; in fact he said he did nothing else. And just before him, there was a young divinity student, just out of college, drove up in an old car of his own. He told me that he was going to hold mission services all the way from Temagami to James Bay. He said there were people up there who never had a chance from one month's end to the other to hear the Word of God – people, he said, living on lonely little lakes and rivers in the woods where practically no one had ever been. I noticed that he had a couple of fishing rods in the back of the car, and a landing net; in fact he showed me a new rod he had, one that folds up; you've seen them I guess; they're called telescope rods. This fellow said that when you get right out like that in the real bush, beyond the Word of God, you need a telescope rod.

There was another fellow, too, an Englishman that I met starting out north, just a fortnight ago. He seemed an awfully aristocratic feller – as a matter of fact he was called the Honourable So and So, but he was all right just the same – you know – nothing wrong with him, except of course his manners were pretty aristocratic, but he couldn't help that . . . and, of course, his way of talking was pretty high-toned . . . yet, do you know, he'd never been educated beyond a public school – he told me so himself – no high school.

This young Englishman was representing a big English investment syndicate. His father, the Earl of Something, is the head of it – a big financier – not a crook, I mean, and was going to get English money put into it, nothing shady about it, perfectly honest deal. His father, as I say, is an Earl, but I met a man who knew him and said that he's all right. Anyway, when this Englishman came down again he said he'd had no time for anything but fishing. He'd been in as far as lake Ohoopohoo. [Do you know it? Well, say!]

But the funny thing is that these visitors going in as such different people, all come out looking the same – all tanned, sunburnt and bitten up with the flies and smeared with bacon and half-ragged – you know, you've been fishing.

But, of course, you must take in French Canada too. . . . There's a sort of old-world charm about it. Go of course first to Montreal – oh, no, you don't need to talk French. The hotels are all English – fine hotels too – English cooking, and you will find that all the shops speak English.

Oh, there's no discomfort to it, just a sense of history. You keep saying to yourself, "Now, I'm in Montreal." Only remember part of it isn't Montreal; it's Westmount, and it's very touchy about it. Still you can say to yourself, "Now I'm in Montreal, unless it's Westmount."

But wait till you see the city of Quebec! Now, there is history for you! Three hundred and thirty-three years old. Yet with one of the most modern hotels in the world. You can sit in the lounge of the Château Frontenac (it's like a sort of terrace overlooking the river); they serve anything you want right there – as I say, you can sit there (after you've given your order) and say:

"Here I am looking at the very view that Count Frontenac looked at, except that it is about a hundred feet higher up than he was, and a little sideways. There, right near the bar, is the place where the American General Montgomery fell – sideways from the bar and a little lower. . . . There's where Wolfe climbed up – behind the bar and about five miles back. The whole thing is what you'd call a panorama. The great Battle of the Plains of Abraham in 1759, that shaped the destinies of this continent, was fought right exactly where you're sitting, but five miles north-west of it. Ask the bar-tender for a picture postcard of it.

Of course you ought to have a look at the rest of French Canada, the Manoir Richelieu at Murray Bay and the Seigneurie on the Ottawa, all English you know – no trouble about French – and with fine golf everywhere, with Scotch professionals and with Irish caddies; oh, French Canada is charming. It's too bad that you won't have time to see much of the Maritimes . . . not only wonderful country but great people. A fine stock, half Yankee loyalists who wouldn't stay home, and half Scottish Highlanders who couldn't.

It made a fine people, and then living as they do, upon fish, that made for brains and so that became their chief industry, the export of brains. They export Presbyterian ministers, college presidents and trustees for banks and financial firms, men who wouldn't steal anything, not even money. They wouldn't steal a cent. I once left one on purpose near one of them. He gave it back, a week later.

But after all, you know, all the time you can spare on your way back should be spent in driving round in this good old province of Ontario – or Upper Canada, as they used to call it. It's the part of Canada most connected with your country and your history and everything. You drive along the St. Lawrence and Lake highways and there's Chrysler's Farm where we licked the Americans, and there's the Stony Creek where the Americans licked us; there's York that they burnt and there's Detroit that we burnt. Things like that make for friendliness. People get to know one another that way.

In fact we've come to realize that in everything but political institutions we are just one people. It was the Americans who settled Upper Canada under the name of United Empire Loyalists.

They brought with them a lot of institutions that are there still – Thanksgiving Dinner and the "little red schoolhouse," the spelling-bee, and the township and all the rest of it. Why, you can go back and forth across the frontier, at Windsor, at Niagara Falls, at Gananoque-Watertown and at Prescott-Ogdensburg, and sample Canadian ale on one side and American lager on the other – till honestly, you can't tell which is which.

But say, come along back to the Midway! That's the bell ringing for the Syrian Girls.

Why Is the United States?

I WONDER how the United States came to be the United States? I mean – how it came to take on its peculiar national character, as a sort of "neighbour" to all the world. As the years and the decades, and now even the centuries have gone past, we can begin to see this peculiar aspect of the United States, unknown anywhere else in history.

It is not imperial dominion; in fact it's not dominion or domination at all – just a peculiar result of mingled merit, destiny and good fortune. People all over the world – Chinese in Chow Chow and Patagonians in Pat Pat – "look to the United States" as a sort of neighbour to appeal to, and to borrow from, just as among the earlier settlers in this country. . . .

Ah! That's it! I see it now – the early settlers. That's where they got it from.

I think there must have been, I mean away back in early settlement times, a country store at a cross-roads – you know the kind of place I mean – a store and post office and farm combined – and this one was called Sam's Place. And the man who kept it, they came to call Uncle Sam.

There were always one or two loafers in the store, sitting on nail-kegs and whittling sticks. Uncle Sam sold pretty well everything, but as a matter of fact the neighbours seemed to do far more borrowing than buying.

In comes a raggedy little girl, very swarthy, with very black hair in pigtails.

"Mister Uncle Sam," she says, "Ma wants the loan of a tea-kettle."

"Now let me see," says Uncle Sam, as he takes a kettle down off a shelf, "which are you? Oh, yes, you're little Guatemala. . . . Here, run along with it. But tell your ma she ain't sent back the last kettle yet."

"Kind o' shiftless folk," says Uncle Sam as she goes out, "they live down below there . . . Spanish . . . fine land for all sorts of stuff they've got, but they don't do anything with it. . . . Sometimes think I might go down there sometime."

Presently in flounces a big dark girl, all colour and style, "Uncle Sam," she says, "let me have another yard of that red calico."

Uncle Sam takes his scissors. "Are you paying for it, Miss Mexico?"

"No, charging it."

"Well, I suppose you got to take it, and tell your pa that I paid him for the coal oil and he hasn't delivered it yet."

Yet Uncle Sam prospered – oh, ever so much! You see, the farm was a wonderful bit of land, and he owned a tannery, and a sawmill – oh, he had everything. Money just seemed to come without trying. "It is a good location," he said.

So of course all the neighbours seemed poor as beside Uncle Sam, and it was just natural that they borrowed his things and charged things and didn't pay, and ate candy (conversation lozenges) out of the open barrel.

He took it easily enough. They were, after all, his neighbours. He treated them all the same way; except that there was one special lot that used to come now and again, who were evidently favourites. These were settled up north and would come down in sleighs in winter and in democrat buggies in summer. "They're folk of my own," says Uncle

Sam, "they settled back north but mebbe they'll come home again some day."

To this good neighbourship there was just perhaps one exception – call it a special case. The reference of course is to old Squire Bull, who lived on a fine, big place, at quite a little distance because it was separated from Uncle Sam's corners by the whole extent of a big mill-pond, so big it was like a lake. From Sam's place you could just see the tops of Squire Bull's grand house and stables.

John Bull was his name and he liked to call himself "plain John Bull," but, as all the neighbours knew, that was just nonsense, for everybody saw that he was "stuck up" and couldn't be "plain" if he tried. Uncle Sam just couldn't get on with him; and that was a funny thing because they were cousins, their folks having originally come from the same part of the country. Sam used always to deny this – at least when he was young. "He's no cousin of mine," he said. Later as he got older, he said, "Mebbe he is," and later still, "Oh, I shouldn't wonder." But he said it grudgingly.

That's the way they lived, anyway, till a reconciliation came about in the queerest way. It happened there came a gang of bandits to the settlement, or, at any rate, the rumour of them. They were reported as robbing here and plundering there. People began to lock up the doors at night – as they never had done before – and you couldn't be sure of travelling the roads in safety. Quite a few had been robbed and one or two killed.

Some people wanted to organize and get together and hunt the bandits down. But Squire John Bull wouldn't believe in the stories about bandits. "All nonsense," he said, "and if any such fellows come round my place they'll get a dose of cold lead."

Uncle Sam didn't do anything either. He was a peaceable fellow, never liking to interfere. "Keep out of quarrels," was his maxim. Yet he had a musket and powder-horn hanging in the store and they said that when it came to shooting he was the best shot in the section.

Well, one day, late in the afternoon, towards dusk, some of the children came rushing breathless into the store. "Mr. Sam, Mr. Sam," they called, "the bandits have come, the gang of bandits. They're over at Squire Bull's place."

"What's that?" said Uncle Sam, all confused.

"The bandits, they're over at Squire Bull's. We saw them smashing in the gates of the yard. We heard the shots. Oh, Mr. Sam, will they kill Mr. Bull?"

"Eh, what?" says Uncle Sam, "smashing in the gates?" – he seemed hesitating. – "Hold on! What's that? By gosh, that's gunshots, I heard them plain."

In ran another child, wide-eyed with fright. "Mr. Sam, come quick, they're over at Mr. Bull's and they've shot some of the help. . . ."

"Is Squire Bull killed?"

"No, he ain't killed. He's in the yard with his back to the wall – his head's all cut – but he's fighting back something awful."

"He is, is he?" said Uncle Sam, and now he didn't hesitate at all. "Hand me down that powderhorn, Sis."

He took the musket off the wall, and he took out of a drawer a six-shooter derringer that no one knew he had.

The children watched him stride away across the field faster than another man would run. Presently they heard shooting and more shots, and then there was silence.

It was just about dark when Uncle Sam came back, grim and dusty, his hands blackened with powder. The children stood around while he was hanging up his musket and his powder-horn.

"Did you get the thieves?" they ventured timidly.

"The gol-darned scoundrels," the old man muttered, "there's some of them won't ever steal again, and the rest will be safe in jail for years to come. Too bad," he added, "some of them came of decent folks, too."

"And how's Squire Bull, is he killed?" the frightened children asked.

"Killed, no, sir!" laughed Uncle Sam, "he's too tough a piece of hickory for that. His head's tied up in vinegar but he's all right. We had a good laugh over it. He allowed I needn't have come but I allowed I won the whole fight. We had quite an argument. But here, don't get in my way, children, hand me that clothes brush and reach me down that blue coat off the peg, the one with the long tails – now that hat."

"But you ain't never going out again, Mr. Sam, are you?"

"Sure, I am. I'm going back over to Squire Bull's. He's giving a party. Now hand me down those cans off that shelf."

And with that Uncle Sam began pulling canned salmon and canned peaches off the store shelves. "I thought I'd bring them along," he said, "that darned old fool – why didn't he say he was getting hard up? I don't believe the folks in his home have been fed right for months. . . . Pride, I suppose! . . . Still he's a fine man, is Squire Bull. My own cousin, you know, children."

The Transit of Venus

The Transit of Venus

A College Story

"AND NOW, gentlemen, that is ladies and gentlemen," concluded Professor Kitter with a slight blush, "having considered the general nature of the Copernican System and the principles underlying it, we shall in our next lecture pass in review the motions of the individual planets, with especial reference to Kepler's Law and the mathematical calculation of their orbits."

Little Mr. Lancelot Kitter, professor of Mathematical Astronomy at Concordia College, had delivered this elegant sentence in much the same form for sixteen years – that is to say, at the close of each opening lecture of the course – and had never been seen to blush over it. But this time he did so. The pink suffusion of his cheeks was visible even without a spectroscope.

Now, there is nothing in the Copernican System to cause a scientist, in these enlightened days, even if he is a bachelor and close on forty, to blush for it. Therefore it must have been something in the class itself.

There were only six students in the class. There was one on the professor's right with a pale face and a head shaped like a bulb, who held a scholarship and had been covering sheet after sheet with mathematical formulae. Professor Kitter had taught him for four years, so the blush couldn't have been for him. There were two students with ruddy faces and long ears who took Astronomy as a "conditioned subject" and wrote notes in diligent despair like distressed mariners working to keep a boat afloat. The blush was evidently not for them.

Then there was Mr. Bill Johnson, otherwise known as "Buck" Johnson, who took Astronomy. It was considered almost as big a "cinch" as the Old Testament, or the president's lectures on Primitive Civilization. All these were recommended by the trainer. Hence Buck Johnson had joined the class and had sat looking at Professor Kitter with the hard irredeemable look of a semi-professional half-back, wondering if he had been wise to take the stuff. But the blush was not for him.

The reason of it was that for the first time in sixteen years there were women in the class. Professor Kitter had never lectured to women before. He did not even know whether to refer to them as "women," "girls," or "ladies."

To the debonair professor of English Literature, who wore a different tie every week, college girls were as familiar as flowers are to the bees. To the elderly Dean of the Faculty they appeared as if merely high school girls. But into the calm precincts of Mathematical Astronomy no women had ever wandered before. Yet there they were, two of them, sitting on the front bench, writing notes and making diagrams of the planets. How daintily their little fingers seemed to draw! From his desk Professor Kitter could see that when Mr. Johnson drew the moon, he drew it in a great, rough circle that even a carpenter would be ashamed of. But when Miss Irene Taylor, the girl with the blue serge suit and the golden hair, drew it, it came out as the cutest little moon that ever looked coquettishly across its orbit at the neat earth.

By the way, Miss Marty, the plain short girl in brown – either brown or scarlet, Professor Kitter hadn't noticed which – may have drawn the moon, too. Very likely she had. It is not part of a professor's duty to observe the figures drawn by the students of the class.

Professor Kitter gave a final bow, gathered up his books, and the class was dismissed.

"How did you like it, Maggie?" said Mr. Johnson to Miss Marty. He called her "Maggie" because they came from the same "home town."

"Fierce, isn't it?" said Miss Marty.

"I almost wish I had taken the Old Testament," said Mr. Johnson dubiously.

"Oh, you can't tell," said Miss Marty, and then she added: "Irene, I don't think you know Mr. Johnson. Let me introduce Mr. Johnson, Miss Taylor."

Mr. Johnson looked at Miss Taylor, and Miss Taylor looked at Mr. Johnson.

"How do you do," they both said.

All of this, however, was happening after Professor Kitter had left the room and he neither saw nor heard it.

A little while after this, the great bell of Concordia College began to toll for afternoon prayers in the college chapel. Whereupon all the population of the college went trooping down the elm avenue without waiting for the prayers, their day's work being done, except, of course, the Professor of Comparative Religion, three students who were officials of the Y.M.C.A., and the two Japanese students of the Sophomore class who were studying Christianity with a view to introducing it into Japan.

Down the avenue walked Miss Taylor in her blue serge suit, and Miss Marty, either in brown or scarlet, and beside them was Professor Kitter, who had joined them at the college door, walking sideways and talking as he went, and bumping into the passers-by, and apologizing.

"I trust, Miss Taylor," he said, "that you were able to understand from today's lecture the general outlines of the Copernican System?"

"Oh, yes," said Miss Taylor, "quite nicely."

The professor didn't ask whether Miss Marty had understood. Miss Marty was short and plain. She could take her chance.

"I was afraid, perhaps, that I hadn't made it quite clear that the sidereal day" – here he bumped into some one else on the other side – "that the sidereal day differs from the solar day merely in the ratio of its fraction of the earth's orbit."

"Oh, yes," said Miss Taylor, and Professor Kitter couldn't but notice what a receptive mind the girl had.

"Of course," he went on, "we are for the moment hampered by our lack of mathematical formulae."

The thought that he and Miss Taylor were hampered – both of them together – gave a new resilience to his step. Miss Marty may have been hampered too. If so, let her look out for herself.

"But later," he said, "we shall call in the calculus to our aid."

No knight ever offered help to a lady with a more chivalrous air.

"Oh, shall we?" said Miss Taylor.

At the foot of the avenue, where it joins the street, the two girls turned off sideways toward the women's residence, and Professor Kitter left them with such a sweeping bow and such Spanish courtesy that an express cart nearly ran over him as he did it. But a mind accustomed to the collisions of the asteroids thinks nothing of these things.

"We shall resume our discussions on Monday," he said. Being a professor, he knew no other form of farewell.

The girls turned a moment and watched him as he disappeared.

"Isn't he the hangedest?" said Miss Marty.

And they both laughed.

That evening, at supper with his maiden sister, Professor Kitter talked so much and so continuously that she wondered what had come over him.

And that night, in the college observatory, where Professor Kitter on a revolving stool gazed at the heavens through a huge telescope, the stars appeared of a brilliance and a magnitude never before witnessed, and Astronomy itself seemed more than ever the noblest and grandest of sciences, and there was such a sweep to the celestial orbit of the moving earth that you could almost hear the heavens humming in glad unison to the rushing movement of it.

So thought and felt Professor Kitter, and with all his science was not aware of the simple thing that had happened to transform the heavens. Yet happened it had, and that swiftly.

For when a man of thirty-eight, who has spent his years since he was seventeen in gazing into the deep blue spaces of the heaven, falls in love, he falls swiftly and far. No lost asteroid seeking in cold space its parent planet falls faster than fell Professor Kitter.

And that same night, while the professor gazed into the sky, Mr. Bill Johnson, of the college football team, took Miss Marty and Miss Taylor to a fifty-cent vaudeville show.

During the months of the college session which followed his opening discourse on astronomy, Professor Kitter – though he was unaware of the fact – lectured to, at, and for Miss Irene Taylor. For her sake he swung the planets round in sweeping orbits. For her sake he projected beams of light into space at the rate of 186,000 miles a second and brought them back to her feet. And for her sake he drew upon the blackboard an equation as long as a snake, seized a bit of chalk, and solved it with the rapidity of a conjurer.

We are told by those who know about such things that the male human being when in love likes to "show off." It appears that this tendency has been evoluted in him through the countless ages of his ascent from the earthworm to the scientist. The male bird displays his brilliant feathers. The nightingale sings. The savage displays his strength. The athlete jumps over a tape.

So what more natural than that a professor of astronomy should call in the heavens to his aid? Professor Kitter practically annexed the whole stellar system to make it show what a man he was.

"You may be surprised to learn," he told the class (he

meant that Miss Taylor might be surprised to learn), "that although a ray of light moves a hundred and eighty-six thousand miles every second, nevertheless, so vast is the distance of open space, the light from our nearest neighbour, Arcturus, takes no less than three years to reach us."

The class were not *really* surprised. College students never are. They have lost the art of it. They merely wrote down "186,000" and "three years" and let it go at that.

"But what shall we say to this fact," continued the professor, "that the light from one of the great spiral nebulae with which we shall become more familiar after Christmas requires for its passage to the earth at this same appalling rate of speed no less than a million years?"

The professor had the right to feel that any girl ought to be impressed by such a fact as this, even though the edge of the effect was taken off by Mr. Johnson looking up from his notes to ask, without any malice, whether the professor had said a million or a billion years. To him it was all the same as long as he got it down right.

Nor was this the only way in which Professor Kitter, unknown to himself, sought to impress the mind of Miss Irene Taylor. His dress during the college session underwent a notable change. Professors as a rule dress queerly. They take no heed of the variations of seasons and of fashions, and their costume knows nothing of the harmony and symmetry of those of the stock-broker or the real estate man.

A professor of Poetry presents perhaps a more flowing appearance, and a professor of Comparative Religion maintains a certain, somber dignity in his dress. But the rank and file of professors of Concordia College wore straw hats in October, morning coats in the afternoon, and Sunday suits on Wednesday with complete indifference.

From this unconsciousness Professor Kitter awoke at the touch of love. His dress, article by article, was transformed. He appeared in a grey suit, brand-new, three-quarters ready, which fitted him admirably so long as the man in the shop gathered up in his hand all the part of it behind the neck and held it. To this was added a brown overcoat that had a red check wandering through it. It was exactly one size too big, but Professor Kitter had been thinking of something else when they tried it on him. He had also bought a new Derby hat that was nearly as shallow as a soup plate, and as a finish to his costume he wore a neat little tartan tie in four colours that must have been designed by its maker for a boy scout at a Scotch picnic. Altered like this the professor felt himself distinctly saucy.

On the first day of this completed costume Professor Kitter met Mr. Johnson and the two girls of the class in the college avenue, and he bowed to them with a sweeping flourish of his hat such as Christopher Columbus used to Queen Isabella.

After he had passed, the three turned and looked at him.

"Ain't he the queer little guy?" said Mr. Johnson.

"Oh, I don't know," said Miss Marty.

Miss Taylor said nothing.

During this same period of time the professor, by a process of rejuvenation similar to his change of dress, had appeared at various college functions at which he had not been present since he was a junior lecturer fifteen years before and had to attend everything that happened. He had sat half-frozen at a hockey match looking at Miss Taylor (seated beside Mr. Johnson) across the rink. He had attended a college play, at which he had also observed Mr. Johnson seated between Miss Taylor and Miss Marty, and he had handed round tea at a perpendicular reception at the president's house, from which he had the pleasure of escorting Miss Marty to the women's dormitory while Mr. Johnson walked beside Miss Taylor. From all of which things Professor Kitter, who prided himself on being an observant man, concluded that Mr. Johnson was greatly improved from what he had been in his lower years, and showed a commendable desire to mingle in society.

Nor was social intercourse the professor's only outlet of

expression. He wrote to Miss Taylor during this period no less than three separate letters. In point of the sentiment that was behind them they were love letters – the first and the last that ever came into the life of the little man – but in form they were far from it.

The first of these letters read:

DEAR MISS TAYLOR,
I fear that I made a rather ridiculous slip in my lecture of this morning in speaking of the proper motion of the sun. I implied that there was a drift of the solar system toward the star Arcturus. I trust that you did not gather from this that there was the least fear of a collision. Let me hasten to correct this error in case it has led to any misunderstanding on your part.

Yours faithfully,
ARTHUR LANCELOT KITTER.

To this reassuring letter the professor received next morning an answer which he opened and read as he sat at breakfast with Miss Catherine Kitter, his maiden sister.

DEAR PROFESSOR KITTER,
I was so much obliged to get your letter about the sun. It was very kind of you to send it, and I am very glad to know that there is not any danger of our colliding with a star.

Very Sincerely,
IRENE TAYLOR.

On reading which the little professor sat lost in bliss – enraptured at the thought that Miss Taylor and he were drifting together through stellar space, while he guarded her against an astronomical disaster.

"Who is your letter from?" asked his sister.

"A note from Miss Taylor," he said, "in regard to the motion of the sun."

On which his sister looked at him through her spectacles with a fixed look in which wonder gradually faded into certainty.

The second letter, which arose in a similar way, dealt

with the retrograde movement of the satellites of Jupiter. The third was concerned with the precession of the equinoxes. To the second Miss Taylor answered, "I was so glad to know about the satellites of Jupiter," and to the third she answered, "I was so glad to know about the precession of the equinoxes."

Teaching so small a group, it was but natural that a professor should find himself from time to time walking down the avenue after the class with one or more of the students. At times Professor Kitter walked down with the student with the head like a bulb, and with him he talked astronomy; in fact, he simply went on with the lecture, the only form of conversation possible between a professor and a student. But sometimes he walked with Miss Marty and Miss Taylor, and once or twice by good fortune he walked with Miss Taylor alone.

Now, by this time he was well aware that there were other things than astronomy that he wanted to say to her ever so much. He wanted to tell her how pretty her cheeks looked in the bright, frosty weather, and how the sun seemed to glint from the snowflakes into her blue eyes, and how cosily the fur that she wore seemed to cling about her neck. This is what he *wanted* to say. But what he *did* say was to tell her that the revolution of the earth is not circular, but around one of the foci of an ellipse.

To which she said, "Oh, is it really?"

Once, as they happened to walk together thus, he had a real chance.

"Isn't it just lovely," Miss Taylor said, "to feel the spring coming?"

Here surely he might have said something real. For instance, he could have told her that to him she was the spring and the sunshine and the flowers all in one, some simple remark of that sort. A first-year student would have said it so easily. Just for a minute he turned and looked at her, and it seemed to Miss Taylor as if he were really about to say something. Perhaps he was. But when he found words what he said was:

"The inclination of the earth upon its axis."

And he knew that he had failed again.

Now, while the college session ran from autumn into winter, and from winter onward toward spring, various other things were happening in and around Concordia College which escaped the notice of Mr. Kitter. One was that Mr. Johnson rang the bell of the women's dormitory – where Miss Marty and Miss Taylor lived – so often that even the hall porter who answered the bell was in no doubt as to why he came. Male students at Concordia were not allowed inside the women's dormitory – except on set occasions as, for example, to listen to a lecture on Palaeontology, which their presence could not contaminate. But nothing prevented them from calling to leave notes or flowers or messages of invitation. In this college session Mr. Buck Johnson was incurring at a local florist's a preferred debt on chrysanthemums that began to look like a German reparation account. Professor Kitter never dreamed of flowers. He would as soon have thought of sending fresh asparagus.

Moreover Mr. Johnson appeared with unfailing regularity in company with Miss Marty and Miss Taylor at all college functions, at the Greek Letter dances, and at the lectures on Relativity and the Y.M.C.A. receptions and the other dissipations of college life.

"The triangle," some gifted wit called them one evening.

"Not much of a triangle about *that*," said another wiser one.

In the Christmas vacation Mr. Johnson and Maggie Marty went off on a train together to their home town, and for ten days Miss Taylor walked alone in the snow. Professor Kitter accidentally joined her as she walked thus, and had the pleasure of explaining to her the nature of the crystallization of the snowflake, which is, of course, nothing more than a simple illustration of the prismatic separation of light. In fact, there is nothing to it.

"The snowflake, Miss Taylor," he said, "is nothing more than a polyhedronal piece of transparent material."

"Oh, is it, indeed?" said Miss Taylor.

As she said it the falling snowflakes were glistening in her yellow hair, and the professor realized again what a wonderful mind the girl had, and how rapidly she grasped scientific phenomena.

Long before, at least two months before the session ended, Professor Kitter knew that he fully intended to ask Miss Taylor to marry him, but he found it impossible to make a beginning. The astronomy had sunk in too deep. Once, when he took her home to the dormitory just at sundown, after hearing an extension lecture on the service of Babylon to the modern world, she stood a moment on the stone steps, her hand in his, to say good night. And the professor said:

"There's something I've been wanting to say, Miss Taylor –" He paused.

She looked into his face, her own illuminated beneath an arc lamp, and said:

"Yes?"

He paused again, struggled, and finally added, "About the orbit of Halley's comet."

On another occasion he actually began, "There are men, Miss Taylor, who –" and again she said "Yes?" but he only repeated "Who, who –" and trailed off into nothingness.

Thus the college year threatened to end with Professor Kitter's love unspoken. But as the day of graduation – the end of all things – drew near, its very nearness gave him resolution. There appeared in prospect a particular occasion when he knew that at least he would have his opportunity, and he meant, at every cost, to use it.

Now, the occasion in prospect was this. It had long been the custom of Professor Kitter to invite his class, hitherto consisting of men, to visit once a year at evening the observatory of Concordia College.

Everybody who knows anything about a college is aware that a class in Astronomy never needs to go out and look at the sky. They can if they want to. The sky is useful in modern astronomy, but it's not necessary. Similarly a class in Dynamics does not need to go and look at machinery, and a class in Money never sees a cent. But it had been for many years the custom of Professor Kitter to invite his class once a year to visit at night the college observatory, of which he was *ex officio* the superintendent.

The observatory was a little round building like a railway water tank and stood beside the Arts Building of Concordia College. In the top room of it there was, among other things, a big, revolving telescope that looked out through a hole in the roof at the sky. Here a man might sit in a moving chair, circling slowly round against the rotation of the earth, his eye exploring into the depths of space, his mind lost in the infinite. Hence he might see the silver desolation of the moon, and the satellites of Jupiter, and Halley's comet once in every seventy-six years, and the transit of Venus once or twice a century. In such surroundings he might attune his mind to the real values of life and to the great things and the little and to what matters and to what does not.

Hitherto once a year came the class in Mathematical Astronomy, clumping up the wooden stairs, not knowing whether to talk in a hush or to laugh out loud. And it was the professor's custom to show the astronomical instruments, to let each student look at the sky, and to repeat each year his regret that the next transit of Venus was not until the year 2004, but he could promise them a total lunar eclipse within sixteen years. Afterward, as a surprise, he produced a tray, duly set and covered by a janitor, on which were sandwiches and ginger-ale and ice-cream – the surprise being no greater than such college "surprises" are when repeated year by year for a generation. On the morning after such occasions the *Daily Concordian* always announced that Professor Kitter had entertained the fourth year class in Astronomy in the tower of the observatory, and that a pleasant time had been had by all.

But this year, as the occasion approached, the professor realized that his fate was to be settled there and then. He would see to it that as they went down from the little tower building he would ask Miss Taylor to be his wife. Somehow the whole thing seemed clear to him beforehand. As if by some psychic process he could see himself in the half-lit curve of the clumsy, circular staircase, with Miss Taylor above, bending down, and he could hear as if by a sort of prescience the very words that he would be saying as he held her hand after she had said "yes" to him.

"I can't tell you what this means to me, Irene. Up till now I never thought of marriage, but now my whole life seems changed."

The little speech went round and round in his mind as if he were rehearsing it, or as if, strangely enough, he had heard some one else saying it – long ago and somewhere else – in a past existence perhaps. In the department of Psychology they talked about such things, and at least two of the professors said that this was possible.

And then all in no time the weeks and the days went by, and the evening was there, and Professor Kitter found himself leading his class up the stairway in the fading twilight of a spring evening and warning Miss Taylor – and even Miss Marty – against the dusk, and apologizing for the stairs, and apologizing for the half mist that might perhaps obscure some of the stars, and apologizing for the transit of Venus being still delayed by nearly a century – apologizing for so many things at once that it seemed odd even to the students.

In the big top room, shaped in a circle, Professor Kitter turned on the light and then showed the students the instruments and explained the rotation of the great telescope that stood in the center of the floor pointed at a hole in the roof beyond which was the gathering darkness of the evening sky. And one by one the students of the class, according to annual custom, sat in the reclining chair and looked upward through the great glass in the depths of the sky and saw a star such as they had never seen before – a star with a face and a disc to it – as silver as a little moon. This,

Professor Kitter explained, was Venus, now beautifully clear in the earlier part of the night being in "partial opposition" and distant only a mere 60,000,000 miles. He explained further, dropping in spite of himself into lecture style, that had it been daylight, and had it been about a hundred years later, and had the telescope been in Madagascar or in the Fiji Islands instead of at Concordia College, and had the atmosphere been suitable, they would have been witnessing a transit of Venus, the most interesting of all astronomical phenomena, in which the planet moves across the face of the sun.

After which Professor Kitter, with such ease of manner as he could assume, discovered his tray of sandwiches and his ginger-ale, and with a good deal of nervousness invited the students to partake of them. So they sat around among the astronomical equipment on improvised seats, the little professor being greatly helped in his efforts by Miss Marty, who had that ease of manner in passing round and accepting sandwiches and drinks which belongs to those from a home town who know nothing of the higher sophistication of city hospitality. Meantime the men students exchanged such learned remarks as, "That is certainly some telescope," and "Venus is certainly some star," and ate steadily and unceasingly, without haste but with no sign of ending.

Then came the end. The girls rose and moved toward the door, but the men of the class, or most of them, went down the dark stairs first to show the way and turn on the lights below. And Miss Taylor, just as Professor Kitter knew she would, went last of all. The professor lingered behind a moment to see that all was right in the observatory; there was still an instrument or two to re-adjust, and there were some readings to make – but these he could postpone till later. When he turned off the light and followed Miss Taylor down the stair, a minute or perhaps two had passed, and in two minutes ever so many things may happen. Certain it is that when Professor Kitter had groped his way down to the first circular landing, there stood on it Mr. Johnson and Miss Irene Taylor. And Mr. Johnson was holding the girl's hand and was saying to her: "I can't tell you what it means to me, Irene. Till now I never thought of marriage –"

But beyond that the little professor heard no more. He made his way upward again to the tower room and waited for a few moments there in the dark, and when he came down again, the students were all down below on the grass outside the building, waiting for the professor to join them.

"I think, if you will permit me, I will say good night here," said the little professor. "I find I have some readings of the instruments to make, and I shall go back for a little while to the observatory."

So they shook hands and thanked him, each in the same words, like a formula. "I certainly enjoyed it very much," – and if there was a certain dreariness in the little professor's voice as he said good night, only one of the class was aware of it.

On which Professor Kitter went back to the tower, and he looked far and deep into the night sky where the things are that never alter and in contemplation of which certain eternal precepts of duty and obligation may be learned. He made his readings of his instruments, and he marked down on a chart his meteorological records of temperature and humidity and pressure. And as he did so, his dreams of the past winter seemed to thread out into thin mist, and he wondered that he had not sooner seen himself as he was, and felt that for him at least the transit of Venus had come and gone.

Professor Kitter went about his tasks of the closing session without hysteria and without complaint. There was for him nothing to say and no one to say it to. But there was still, at least, his work, and even if a man is close on forty, and small of size, and no fit companion for the life and gaiety of youth, there are still equations to be worked out left over from the last lunar eclipse, and by these navigation may be aided and human progress set a little further on. Professor Kitter knew nothing of such things as the "theory of duty" and such ideas as the "subordination of self as a factor in social survival." These things were taught in another department and were optional even to students. But the professor worked at his lunar equations and went about his work, quiet and unnoticed.

Only once his mind was brought to a sudden and painful attention. It was on a certain day in graduation week, when the examinations were over and nothing was left but to wait for Commencement Day, while meantime each day was filled with student celebrations – valedictory meetings of classes, the presentation of an old English play out on the grass by the youngest of the graduates in English, afternoon receptions on the lawn of the president's house, and dinners, so-called, where vast quantities of celery and ice-cream were consumed. It was in this week that the little professor, entering the committee room of the faculty, heard the head of his faculty, Dean Elderberry Foible, venting his opinions with his usual emphasis. And he was talking of student marriages such as happened now and then immediately after graduation.

"Absolutely preposterous!" said the Dean. "Ridiculous! Ought not to be allowed. Mere children" – all students seemed children to Dean Foible – "getting married before they know the first thing of life. There should be something to forbid it in the curriculum, or it ought to need at least the consent of a vote of the faculty. And a young fellow like Johnson," the Dean went on, "why, he's only twenty-three! Just because his great-uncle or somebody has left him a little money and he is able to get married – pooh! preposterous!"

Of that speech Professor Kitter heard no more. He gathered up his letters and left. Nor did he hear any more of the subject matter of which the dean spoke till the very afternoon of graduation day. But on that day he was walking up the avenue among the elms, and as he walked he encountered, fully and fairly and unavoidably, Miss Irene Taylor. Even a professor's eye could see that she was dressed for an occasion.

He would have raised his hat and passed, but she stopped him. It was plain that she meant to stop him.

"Why, Professor Kitter!" she exclaimed. "Aren't you coming to the wedding?"

The professor stammered something. "Did you mean to say that you didn't know?" Miss Taylor went on.

The professor muttered something to the effect that he had heard something.

"Oh, I thought everybody knew. Why, Maggie Marty and Mr. Johnson are to be married at three o'clock, and you know it's just lovely! He's come into quite a lot of money from some forgotten uncle or somebody, and they're going to go to Paris and both study over there – I forget what it is that they are going to study, but they say that there are ever so many courses you can study now in Paris. Why, didn't you know? He asked her on the way over to the observatory that night, and he told me all about it going down the stairs as we went out. Oh, you really must come down to the church anyway, even if you don't go to the house. Maggie said they wrote and asked you. Do come!"

And with that she put her hand on the little professor's arm and turned him in her direction.

What Professor Kitter said as they went down the avenue is not a matter of record. It may have concerned the altitude of the sun, which seemed all of a sudden to have leaped to a surprising height and brilliance, or it may not. But at least it was effective, and when after the wedding and the ceremony that went with it, the two walked away together under the elm trees, it was understood that Miss Taylor, after an interval shorter than anything ever heard of before in astronomy, was to become the professor's wife. And it transpired further that she had kept all her notes in class from the very start, and that she had copied a whole equation off the board because he wrote it, and that his letter about the proper motion of the sun had seemed to her the sweetest letter she had ever dreamed of.

All of which things rapidly become commonplace. Especially as Miss Taylor is now Mrs. Arthur Lancelot Kitter, and attends college teas, and reads little papers on Chinese Philosophy at the Concordia Sigma Phi Society – and, in fact, acts and behaves and seems much as any other professor's wife.

Migration in English Literature

Migration in English Literature

A Study of England and America

All lovers of Dickens will recall with delight, as readers of *David Copperfield*, the final destiny of Mr. Micawber as an emigrant to Australia. That unbeatable gentleman, always waiting for something to "turn up," found it at last turn up in the Antipodes. There is a triumphant passage in which is described "the public dinner given our distinguished fellow-colonist and townsman, Wilkins Micawber, Esquire, Port Middlebay, district Magistrate." We are told that the dinner "came off in the large room of the hotel, which was crowded to suffocation, it being estimated that no fewer than forty-seven persons were accommodated with dinner at one time." We are told further that when Mr. Micawber's health was proposed, "the cheering with which the toast was received defied description; again and again it rose and fell like the waves of the ocean." I don't think that Charles Dickens himself knew whether this description of the ovation to Mr. Micawber was to be taken as burlesque or as poetic justice; whether he is laughing at Mr. Micawber, converted, after all his grandiose idcas, into a large toad in a small puddle, or exulting in the idea of his final vindication as a man of exception. If we could ask Dickens we should be no further on; he'd claim it both ways at once.

But this characteristic passage opens wide the gate of reflection; here is the path that leads into a very garden of discovery. This outgoing of the people of England, spread over three centuries, how did it react upon the life and thought of the mother country? Migration in the past was not the mere transit of our day, with its easy and frequent return and its voices across the ocean. Emigration meant farewell. When the anchor had been lifted with the capstan turned by all hands, singing in chorus, when the white cliffs of the English coast sank dim on the horizon, that was good-bye. And in that leave-taking was all the poignancy of final parting, all that goes with the prospect of unknown exile, but for younger hearts all that goes with the dawn of larger hopes. Can we wonder that the joy and sorrow, the hope and the tragedy of the outgoing emigrant sets its stamp deep on the literature of England?

The theme suggested, at least to my relative ignorance, is one but little exploited in our histories. We have, I think, all too little realized the reaction of America on British life and character. We are so accustomed to think of British America, past and present, as the child of England, that we fail to see that England, in a sense, is the child of America. It was the great voyages of the sixteenth and seventeenth centuries that reanimated the sea-faring spirit of England. People learned to know and love their homeland by their losing it awhile. The blood of Vikings moved again the veins of Sussex farmers. Courage fallen asleep or latent in sheltered farmsteads woke again to something fiercer and less civilized in men who lived among dangers and slept among savages. The boys who for three centuries ran away to sea, the dispossessed younger sons who blew like thistle-down over the newer lands, the Covenanters martyred to the West Indies, and, in the Victorian age, the outgoing singing poor, crowded and dirty and triumphant – all these in their going and in their casual returns, in the magnet attraction of their new hopes, the glamour of their new fortunes – all of these helped to fashion, to remake, the character of England as we know it. Those of us who preceded or followed Mr. Micawber to new dominions, I speak here collectively for uncounted millions of us, dead or alive, can in a sense say of England, "We too made it."

But I am discussing here not the whole field of the reaction of migration on life and character, but only of the reflection and evidence of it as seen in our imagination. It appears as a major theme in our poetry – mostly in its aspect of the sorrow of parting, but at times with a note of joy. It breaks into our earlier romantic literature as an element of adventure, and when romance widens into the broad current of nineteenth-century fiction – the thing called the novel – the idea, one might say, also, the *device* or expedient of migration runs like a thread in the woven cloth. Elsewhere emigration appears as a sort of defeatist solution of social problems just beginning. To go somewhere else is a fine way of avoiding trouble at home.

I do not think that we shall find much of the theme suggested in the literature – the plays or the prose and the poetry; there were no novels – of the heroic age of exploration and discovery itself. Thomas More's *Utopia* (1516) was written before migration began. It professed to be and has turned out to be nowhere. Shakespeare died before the outgoing of the English people had gone further than John Smith's Virginia. In the play *King Lear*, the noble Kent, banished by the foolish old king, declares that he will "seek liberty in new lands," but by that he hardly means that he is going to settle in the United States; or at best Kent merely anticipates in his words ideas destined to germinate later on – a habit, it appears, with Shakespeare. So, too, when the admirable enthusiast Richard Hakluyt gathered from mariners and manuscripts his priceless *Principal Navigations* (1589), the inspiration was rather towards the mastery of the sea than of the land. Those who went over the sea in those earlier days went as adventurers minded to return.

There were no "emigrants" in the sorrowing sense of people going to a new home in the wilderness until the outgoing of the Puritans. They carried in their hearts, in spite of persecution, all their love and longing for the country they had left. "We do not say," such are the memorable words of Mather, one of the Pilgrim ministers, "farewell, Babylon, farewell, Rome – but farewell, dear England." But the mind of the Puritans, in America as at home, was not cast in the mould of imaginative literature. For them truth overwhelmed fiction, and the pretty fancies of poetry and of play-acting were alike of the devil. It was the well-worn Psalm-book of Ainsworth, and not the latest Italian novella, that lay on the lap of Priscilla when John Alden came on his vicarious courting. They did not write of their sorrows. The first fruits of their printing press were *The Bay Psalm Book* and such volumes as *The Wonder Working Providence of Zion's Saviour in New England*. Similarly, in so far as the outgoing of the Puritans reacted upon English thought, it affected the religious rather than the literary aspect of the mind of England.

It is not, I imagine, till the eighteenth century when emigration to a new home, definite and final, was becoming an accepted feature of English life, that we begin to trace its mark in literature. Yet it is notable that even Gray's *Elegy* of 1753 shows no trace of it. The rude forefathers of the hamlet sleep beneath their elms; but they are all there; the count is complete; there are no vacant places. The destiny of the mute inglorious Miltons and the English Hampdens was still at home. But compare a century later Mrs. Hemans' *Graves of a Household* – in which all are gone; the "blood red fields of Spain," the "blue lone sea," the "forests of the west" have claimed them. Mrs. Hemans was never in America. But when she wrote:

> One in the forests of the west
> By a dark stream is laid,
> The Indian knows his place of rest,
> Far in the cedar shade,

the imagery strikes with wonderful truth any who have ever seen it. The "darkness," the heavy shadow of the cedars, is as characteristic as the silence that goes with a forest of pine. But even Mrs. Hemans' thought is rather that of the break-up of an English home by war and overseas adventure than the allied subject of separation by migration to a new land. The latter, one might say, is in a sense the higher theme. The deepest notes of human tragedy are those that sound from human fate and not from human wrong. Such notes convey the thought of tragedy where no one is to blame, the injustice of tyranny does not enter, but only the crushing weight of human destiny – nobody's fault.

Compare here the memorable passage in Robert Louis Stevenson's memorable book *Kidnapped*. It is an incidental description of an emigrant ship from the west coast of the Highlands in the period just after the rising of 1745:

> As we got a little nearer . . . there began to come to our ears a great sound of mourning, the people on board and those on shore crying and lamenting, one to another, so as to pierce the heart. Then I understood this was an emigrant ship bound for the American colonies. . . . The exiles leaned over the bulwarks, weeping and reaching out their hands. . . . But at last the captain of the ship, who seemed near beside himself (and no great wonder) in the midst of the crying and confusion, came to the side and begged us to depart. . . . The chief singer in our boat struck into a melancholy air, which was presently taken up by both the emigrants and their friends on the beach, so that it sounded from all sides like a lament for the dying. I saw the tears run down the cheeks of the men and women in the boat, even as they bent at the oars; and the circumstances and the music of the song (which is one called "lochaber no more") were highly affecting.

This same crushing sorrow of the exile, as opposed to the wistful regret of the voluntary settler, is voiced by Swinburne in his *Jacobite's Exile*, "bonnier shine the braes of Tyne, than a' the fields of France." But in a generation or two of children, exile and settler are all one, their common lot blending to a common thought.

With the sorrow of parting, acute and for the moment

overwhelming, is to be set the homesickness, the unending longing for "home" that never dies. It was never better expressed than in the stanza:

> From the lone shieling on the misty island
> Mountains divide us and the waste of seas –
> Yet still the blood is strong, the heart is Highland,
> And we in dreams behold the Hebrides.

The verse appeared in *Blackwood's Magazine* of 1829, as one of the stanzas of a poem generally understood to be written by John Galt, the moving spirit of the Canada Land Company, founder of our city of Guelph. Those who know the verse never forgot it. Nor does it matter if the reader doesn't know what shieling means. I know it, but I won't tell; it isn't necessary. I liked the poem almost better when I didn't know. The dim uncertain meanings of terms half understood heighten the colour of imagination as in the reading of a child.

But compare the wistful pathos and the mutual affection of the "misty island" with the background of Oliver Goldsmith's *Deserted Village*. Here is contrast indeed. "Sweet Auburn, loveliest village of the plain, where health and plenty cheer the labouring swain," has been half depopulated by the rapacity of greedy landlords and the brutality of new wealth. Its people are driven abroad, not as to new and happier homes in a newer England, but as destined to die in a region of horror:

> Ah, no! To distant climes, a dreary scene,
> Where half the convex world intrudes between,
> Through horrid tracts with fainting steps they go,
> Where wild Altama murmurs to their woe.

This "horrid" place (only classical students appreciate that word), the reader will be "horrified" to find, was the (present) State of Georgia, at that time (1769) the scene where General Oglethorpe's new paradise had gone a little to the bad. One can redeem the reputation of "the Palmetto State," however, by dropping rapidly down the decades to

Wordsworth's *Ruth* (of 1800). Here both migration and Georgia appear in a different light – the temptation of elopement to a savage paradise. Ruth, a "village maiden" (type now killed by education), has met a

> . . . Youth from Georgia's shore,
> A military casque he wore,
> With splendid feathers drest;
> He bought them from the Cherokees;
> The feathers nodded in the breeze . . .

He is not himself an Indian, but Wordsworth says in a truly Wordsworthian line, "He was a lovely youth. I guess." I guess so too. At any rate, he told Ruth about Georgia in words that would adorn an up-to-date Tourist Handbook:

> He told of the magnolia spread
> High as a cloud, high overhead!
> The cypress and her spire;
> Of flowers that with one scarlet gleam
> Cover a hundred leagues and seem
> To set the hills on fire!

Ruth plans to elope, is deserted, goes mad, and another bad mark is set against colonial settlement. But all this stuff is harmless from its very ignorance.

The closing years of the eighteenth century and the opening of the nineteenth found little room for the emigrant. The air was loud with battle, the sky lurid with a conflict that outlasted a generation. Literature responded to the thrills of war. Poetry sang of "Nelson and the North" and of the "Mariners of England" who defied the "battle and the breeze." The favourite interjection was "Ho!" and not "Alas!" Even the appearance of the "professional" convict, with Captain Phillip's Botany Bay enterprise of 1787–88, passed for the time unnoted as a theme of literature. Yet it was there. Before that day convicts had gone out in an unending series as "indentured labourers" to America. Indeed, America, through the voice of Benjamin Franklin, speaking as "Poor Richard" in his *Almanac*, had already protested against their presence. But the independence of the United States brought with it a resolute and very successful determination on the part of the Americans to supply their own criminals. Hence, scarcely noted among greater things, the convict ships and the convict settlements became a part of the British environment. Later on it broke into literature. But the poetry of the moment found no place for it. A slight exception here is found in Southey's four poems, the *Botany Bay Eclogues*, 1794, a sort of rogues' gallery of loneliness and misery – of souls broken with crime and cruelty, finding at last even in the "barbarous climes where angry England sends her outcast sons" the "saving hand of grace," the soothing touch of eternal nature.

With the nineteenth century appears in our literature of migration the sorrows of Ireland, a cup of misery, as the Irish have said, that has been overflowing for generations and is not full yet. The most notable, of course, of the Irish singers was Thomas Moore, much of whose work is as alive today as ever. Mutilated by school recitations, massacred at a thousand pianos, the words still haunt, the melodies still sound. The reason is that Moore's work was wonderfully and typically Irish – the wistful regret for things that have been and are not, regret that things must ever end, or that they don't begin, a kind of satisfied dissatisfaction with life. Said in English it sounds like grumbling. Said in Irish it is called a "lament" and connects somehow with the pathos of natural scenery and the rippling music of words. Compare Father Prout: "the bells of Shandon that sound so grand on the pleasant waters of the river Lee."

Moore himself came to America in 1804, and drew, during his visit, out of our woods and rivers the same magic as from Ireland. Every one knows his *Canadian Boat Song*:

> Faintly as tolls the evening chime
> Our voices keep tune and our oars keep time;
> Soon as the woods on shore look dim

We'll sing at St. Anne's our parting hymn.
Row, brothers, row, the stream runs fast,
The rapids are near and the daylight's past.

Naturally Moore, even as an amateur immigrant, strikes the note of sorrow of the real one. Compare such a passage:

As slow our ship her foamy track
Against the wind was cleaving
Her trembling pennant still look'd back
To that dear Isle 'twas leaving. . . .

Or Thomas Irwin (1823–92):

The white sails are filled and the wind from the shore
Blows sad from the hills we shall visit no more, etc. . . .

Naturally the song of Irish emigration was especially connected with the idea not only of leaving Ireland but of finding a new home in the United States. These, we recall, were the days of the "melting-pot" of the "land of liberty" before the words "quota" and "deportation" had come into our language. An Irish poet (Maurice Fitzgerald) therefore could weep (c. 1880) over "Moonlight on New York Bay," the poignancy of the situation being that the moon might very probably be shining also on Tipperary:

O beautiful moon, art thou shining tonight
On the green hills of Ireland, away, far away?

But the real pathos of Irish migration to America was never more wonderfully expressed than by Lady Dufferin in her song depicting the outgoing emigrant leaving Ireland after the death of his young wife and her child:

I'm sittin' on the stile, Mary,
Where we sat side by side
On a bright May mornin', long ago,
When first you were my bride.
The corn was springin' fresh and green,
And the lark sang loud and high

And the red was on your lip, Mary,
And the love-light in your eye. . . .

They say there's bread and work for all,
And the sun shines always there –
But I'll not forget old Ireland
Were it fifty times as fair.

The pathos of the bereaved immigrant of a hundred years ago is now lost for us today in the wider pathos of the words "bread for all, the sun shines always there" – the pathos of the broken hopes of a continent.

As contrasted with the Irish "lament" the typical English poem or song of nineteenth-century migration is of a sturdier character, more stress on hope, less grumbling, and less scenery. Naturally so. The British were the dominant lot; for half a century the least of them in coming to Canada had a notion that he owned it. And if the iron of disappointment entered their souls (see Mrs. Moody's *Roughing It in the Bush*) they did not turn it into poetry. The typical English song was the one that ran:

Cheer, boys, cheer; no more of idle sorrow.
Courage, true hearts, will bear us on our way.
Hope points before and shows a bright tomorrow;
Let us forget the darkness of today.

The song went on to explain that the "star of the Empire glitters in the West." If this means Saskatchewan and Alberta the proposition is open to doubt. But the song carried inspiration. It was the "up anchor" song of the outgoing ships. I heard it first on the deck of the *Sarmatian?* A.D. 1876, in helping to haul on a rope which I understood was lifting the anchor. It is much superior to the jazz music of an up-to-date liner's orchestra playing till the bar opens. We need new poets.

All of this so far has dealt with poetry, the morc adaptable vehicle for the purpose. One turns to emigration as in prose, in fiction. Here the theme presents a strange medley of pathos and miracle, final eclipse and sudden fortune, an artifice of total disappearance or a conjuror's trick of sudden and glorious resurrection. No one used this theme – at times, this artifice – more than did Charles Dickens. He was in a sense preoccupied with it. As a young man in the romantic age of resentment and illusion he cherished a hatred of English "Toryism" – a natural feeling in a "genius," poor, unrecognized, and unknown to Tories. He dreamed of "giving it all up" – every young man decides to give it all up. He had his eye on Tasmania. But instead of that the sudden illumination of fortune that came with the *Pickwick Papers* enabled him, in 1842, to visit America. After that, England suited him forever. But there remained in his mind, if only by way of literary furniture – as in a large house ready for any kind of entertainment – the notion of migration. Indeed, he "migrated" his sons. Charles, the eldest son, was sent, for a while, to Hong Kong to learn colonial trade. Alfred Tennyson Dickens went out to settle in Australia. Francis, the third son, went to North-West Canada, became an officer in the Mounted Police, and was in Battleford during the Rebellion of 1885.

Naturally then if Dickens migrated his own family, *a fortiori* he was willing to migrate his literary creations. Along with the classic case of Mr. Micawber is that of Dr. Mell, the erstwhile schoolmaster present at the same banquet, but dug up from so far back in *David Copperfield* that the reader has forgotten who he is; but whoever he was or is, he is now endowed with a daughter, evidently destined to marry Mr. Micawber's gifted son, Wilkins, Junior! Thus does Dickens use the rapid light and shadow of emigrant fortune to illuminate his closing horizon. Still more characteristic of Dickens and of all the Victorians is the use of migration as a means of redemption. Young Charlie Bates, a convicted thief in *Oliver Twist*, lives to become the "merriest drover in New South Wales." Martin Chuzzlewit "sees the light" among the mosquitoes of the Mississippi.

As with Dickens so with the general crowd of mid-Victorian writers. Thackeray in his *Virginians* proposes a wider field, the contrast between the branch of a family that stays at home and the branch that migrates to Virginia, a study "of opposing loyalisms and severing patriotisms." Thackeray proposed this, but got so busy talking to the reader about anything and everything that he forgot about it. Nodding over his patchwork he stitched in some good pieces of eighteenth-century London, and used Indians and redcoats to colour Virginia.

It is difficult to cite individual examples of characters in fiction with any sustained interest for the reader. The lapse of time, the change of taste, the higher gear of modern life have removed the books of three generations ago from the generality of the present public. Who among them knows or cares how many characters migrated overseas out of the works of Miss Edgeworth or Charles Lever or Whyte-Melville or Wilkie Collins? But the statement may stand that from the pages of Victorian fiction there passed out an unending procession of unfortunates to seek redemption or oblivion in new lands.

But what is difficult of proof, without loss of interest, in dealing with half-forgotten authors becomes so simple as to be redundant when we turn to authors within easy reach of memory and still within easy hearing of their audience. One has but to name Kipling to call up a succession of gentleman-rankers, of forgotten men, of "men who were," men who "would be kings"; or to name Robert Louis Stevenson to think of Oxford graduates quoting Latin on South Sea Islands, or Masters of Ballantrae in the American wilderness; or Conan Doyle with his Refugees; while in the full glare of modern publicity and with the full rapidity of modern transport, such happy writers as Mr. Phillips Oppenheim fill their pages with mystery-men, disappearing in the forest or jungle, to reappear, fabulously rich, in a London restaurant, ordering – think of it – Martini cocktails! For here is another note, and a happy one, happier than the mere negation of oblivion or the cold light of moral reform – that of exiles returning dripping with diamonds, covered with rubber, or heavy with gold.

There is a perennial human interest in disappearance and return. Even Enoch Arden, broken and penniless, became a village sensation. But a return accompanied by great wealth, to be shared by a grateful family, that is something else. Oddly enough it is the French – see Alphonse Daudet – and not ourselves, who have recognized so clearly this type of the returning millionaire as, to give him a name, *L'oncle di'Amérique*. But beside his sunlit figure the shadow falls upon a darkened one, especially known in fiction, that of the returned convict. As the penal settlements grew from the first establishment of Botany Bay to a system that threw its shadow over an empty island continent, the convict began to come into literature; the convict, with all the mixture of pity and terror that went with his lot; the hulks where he waited his departure, the convict ship that carried him, and the unknown fate – beyond human ken, over the edge of the world – that swallowed him up. *For the Term of his Natural Life* – so runs the grim title of Marcus Clarke's great story. With it and after it were many others. The theme had all the attraction of unknown terror. The "convict" idea fascinated a generation with its horror.

Strangely enough, slavery and the slave trade never got into our literature in their own day – except in one fierce burst of denunciation as a ground-swell of the coming American Civil War. Longfellow's poem of the slave, an African king, dying "beside the ungathered rice," and the book *Uncle Tom's Cabin*, on whose pages fell the tears of a myriad of children; these came not as literature in the pure sense but from the driving urge of anger and political passion. But the deeper disgrace is that the slave went unwept in our literature till the thing was over. The flag of which the Victorians, after 1833, used to sing that it "never shall float o'er a slave," had perhaps floated over more slaves, in its time at sea till 1807 and on land till 1833, than any flag in the world. But the slavery motive was what the psychoanalyst would call a mixed complex; the tragedy had got mixed with white superiority, with the Bible, and with West Indian fortunes. The dominant race cannot voice its victims; and the negroes could not sing that sort of song.

But the convict was different. He was white and, therefore, a tragedy and fit for literature. As the "ticket of leave" system developed, the convict turned into a kind of immigrant. His restored fortune put him, as literature, alongside of the "American uncle"; indeed there was even a jocular touch available with him. "True patriots all; for be it understood, we left our country for our country's good," so sang once an actual and gifted Australian ex-convict. Such a person naturally became an ingredient in the "historical" fiction dealing with a country like Australia, lucky enough to have no history. It is amazing what has been done with so little. In Canada with romance and history broadcast over our country, how little we have done with it!

There remains one enthusiastic page over which migration and settlement is written in large and half-formed letters – the boy's books of the bygone century. This section of our literature has stamped the idea of migration on the mind not of the nation at large but of the rising generation, or rather of the successive generations that have risen in turn for two hundred years. These are the "boys' books" that deal with refugees on desert islands, with "settlers" in the wilderness, with the ingenious building of shelters in trees and snug igloos in the snow. Here is all the charm that goes with "contrivance"; with the surmounting of difficulty, with the "creation," as it were, of economic life.

The parent book is, of course, the immortal *Robinson Crusoe*, a book which probably Defoe himself did not understand. Such is often the way with authors. Dickens failed to appreciate Mr. Pickwick for many instalments and Conan Doyle grew bitter against Sherlock Holmes, not realizing that he had created in Sherlock and Watson far more endearing characteristics than mere scientific deduction. So with Defoe. He meant to present Crusoe as an outcast, an unfortunate object of pity. Crusoe "fooled" him, so to say, and became an object of envy to generations of English boys. Cowper tried later on to sing of Crusoe (under his own name of Alexander Selkirk) in terms of compassion.

> Oh, Solitude, where are the charms
> That sages have seen in thy face?
> Better dwell in the midst of alarms
> Than reign in this horrible place.

Cowper, as a boy sees it, misses the point. Think of Crusoe, with his fertile island full of yams, breadfruit, and coconuts, his axe to build a house with and wild goats to make umbrellas of, and presently his devoted Friday to attend and serve him! Can you better that? Note especially the "devoted native" theme which has attracted uncounted thousands of English boys and helped to give the world the "faithful Sambo," the "Gunga Dins" – these are the stuff that dreams, boys' dreams, are made on, and out of the dreams of boys may grow the achievements of a nation.

Robinson Crusoe is the type. But it is followed by a long succession of "boys" books (some boys are seventy years old) dealing with the creative effort of isolated settlers, a series that has only died out when the world has become full, and is now being transferred to the moon. One recalls with affection the Victorian stories of R. M. Ballantyne of the Hudson's Bay Company, chief interpreter to England of the unknown north. Such books are not of adventure. Leave adventure to the "Spanish Main," crowded with pirates and French privateers and sailing-ships abandoned with no one on board but a beautiful girl and an old man. That's all right. But it belongs to a different kind of story. Even in *Robinson Crusoe*, to a boy's mind, the "adventure" comes in as a disturbance; the "fun" is the settlement, or rather not so much "fun" as a sense of "snugness," a self-satisfaction. Oddly enough, some of the favourite books of this type for English boys were written by foreigners. Just as Hans Andersen and the Brothers Grimm [illegible] our fairy stories, so the author of the *Swiss Family Robinson* and Jules Verne, as the author of *The Mysterious Island*, wrote our best "settlement" stories. The Swiss Family stuff is a little tame, everything too easy – for the nursery rather than the boarding-school. It was written by Johann Rudolf Wyss, a Swiss professor of philosophy who knew as much about desert islands as a Swiss professor of philosophy would. In any case, to a boy's mind, having the "family" there at all spoils it. When you strike an A1 desert island you don't want father and mother. But Jules Verne's story hits it just right; the landing from a balloon on an empty and remote, but very fertile, island; the group of cheerful and ingenious men (how cheerful they are – but boys never notice that) who start bare-handed from nothing and contrive everything – what a wonderful setting! All machines can be operated backwards, put into "reverse gear," so to speak. So it often is with literary composition. The reverse gear of Robinson Crusoe is Enoch Arden. There he sits, poor long-haired exile in the Pacific sunset, weeping for home. He won't even cut his hair, not appreciating the fun of "contriving" a pair of scissors out of oyster-shells. No contrivance for him. But notice, even in his very tears, how his sorrows call up a picture of England as if to make us feel that we have never loved it enough:

> The climbing street, the mill, the leafy lanes,
> The peacock yew-tree and the lonely Hall,
> The horse he drove, the boat he sold, the chill
> November dawns and dewy-glooming downs,
> The gentle shower, the smell of dying leaves,
> And the low moan of leaden-coloured seas.

So too with all the emigrants. I think it has often been the people in this exile of settlement who have loved England best, who still, after twenty years, talk of "home," and see it as things only can be in retrospect of time and in the magic of distance. The stuff that binds the British Empire is not texts and tariffs, but such back and forward reactions.

"*J'en passe et des meilleurs*," as the French say when

they run out of examples. Let me under that pretext turn to the use of migration, not in the realm of fancy, but in the equally imaginary world of nineteenth-century economics. I am willing to call it, if not a world of the imagination, at any rate a lost world or a world that never came true. Political economy is not, or should not be, a work of the imagination, and hence lies properly outside the scope of the present discussion. But there is an odd parallel as between the use of the emigrant in fiction as a sort of defeatist method of getting rid of undesirables, and the classical economic use of the "emigrant man" as a defeatist solution of social problems at home. Into their imagined setting the "emigrating economic man" was placed as a sort of safety-valve. If there were too many at home he was supposed to get out. The world which seemed very empty then was all his. He was supposed to care nothing about flags, loyalty, and allegiance. At the very time – in the opening Victorian years – when the Canada Company was embarking emigrants to Upper Canada, another organization, the Colombian Society, was undertaking to send them to Venezuela.

It remained for one of the interpreters of the classical economics to prove this parallel between the defeatist migration of the economist and the "redemption" migration of the novelist by bridging over the gap between them and turning economics into fiction. Harriet Martineau (1802–76) had an active mind. She was as optimistic as sunshine, as exact as a checkerboard, and about as original as a hen. Her sunshine was refracted by the prism of class and caste that turned the world into masters and servants, gentle and simple, doing their duty in the state of life into which the rubric of the catechism called them. But she had an ingenious facility of words and a concrete presentation that could turn simple things into stories. On this basis she undertook to rewrite the immovable truths of the dismal science as a series of Tales – *Illustrations of Political Economy* in nine volumes. The Tales are among the curiosities of literature, and as humour they deserve to rank with

Sandford and Merton and Archibald Marshall's *Birdikin Family*. In volume IV is found Tale No. 10, which deals with migration under the title of "New Homes." In this bright little narrative a Kentish family go out to Van Dieman's Land (see under Tasmania), the father and mother and Frank and Ellen, the older brother and sister as indentured servants, and two younger boys, their half-brothers Bob and Jerry, lucky fellows, as convicts. It seems that Bob and Jerry had "beaten up" (*more Americano*) two young gentlemen, for which they were to be hanged but were let off with transportation. Today they would have got three months, or in America have "bumped the young gentlemen off" and got nothing. Here is the cheerful landing of the family – home ties are nothing to them – in the Antipodes:

> Ellen was the first of the family that arrived at Hobart Town. Next came the convict ship which was sent round to Launceston. Next the batch of parish immigrants arrived and Frank found, on application to the proper government officer, that his sister had landed in good health, and had received a high character from the clergyman and his lady who had come over as superintendents of the expedition; and had been forwarded to a district where a service had been procured for her as dairy-maid on a settler's farm; and that care had been taken that her parents and her brother should be indentured to farmers in the same neighbourhood. So far, all was well.

Quite so, in fact, fine. One can easily see how Frank and Ellen become prosperous settlers regarded with approval by the "gentry" who come out later. The convict brothers also flourish. Bob becomes a sort of convict labour boss and then independent. Jerry, on ticket of leave, takes on a "black wife," refuses to work and lives apparently by pillaging the "gentry." We have a last vision of him leaving the Island, as too small for his activities. The moral is that the colonies need more gentry, more servants, and, as Miss Martineau says herself, that "our convict arrangements tend to the further corruption of the offender by letting him experience a great improvement in his condition as a direct consequence of his crime." How much better to keep him in jail for life!

Such has been the lot of the emigrant. Cast out in our history by persecution as a refugee, by economics as a superfluity, he might well have disappeared into limbo. In place of which, as the Latin poet would say, "*tamen usque recurrit*." Literature brings him back as an uncle from America, an empire builder, or at least as the point and moral of a tale.

Three Score and Ten

Three Score and Ten

The Business of Growing Old

OLD AGE is the "Front Line" of life, moving into No Man's Land. No Man's Land is covered with mist. Beyond it is Eternity. As we have moved forward, the tumult that now lies behind us has died down. The sounds grow less and less. It is almost silence. There is an increasing feeling of isolation, of being alone. We seem so far apart. Here and there one falls, silently, and lies a little bundle on the ground that the rolling mist is burying. Can we not keep nearer? It's hard to see one another. Can you hear me? Call to me. I am alone. This must be near the end.

I have been asked how old age feels, how it feels to have passed seventy, and I answer in metaphor, as above, "not so good."

Now let us turn it round and try to laugh it off in prose. It can't be so bad as that, eh, what? Didn't Cicero write a book on old age to make it all right? But you say he was only just past sixty when he wrote it, was he? That's a tough one. Well, what about Rabbi ben Ezra, you remember – "Grow old along with me." Oh, he was eighty-one, eh? No, thanks, I'll stay right here around seventy. He can have all his fun for himself at eighty-one.

I was born in Swanmoor, a suburb of Ryde in the Isle of Wight, on December 30, 1869. That was in Victorian England at its most Victorian, far away now, dated by the French Empire, still glittering, and Mr. Dickens writing his latest book on the edge of the grave while I thought out my first on the edge of my cradle and, in America, dated by people driving golden spikes on Pacific railroads.

It was a vast, illimitable world, far superior to this – whole continents unknown, Africa just an outline, oceans never sailed, ships lost over the horizon – as large and open as life itself.

Put beside such a world this present shrunken earth, its every corner known, its old-time mystery gone with the magic of the sea, to make place for this new demoniac confine, loud with voices out of emptiness and tense with the universal threat of death. This is not mystery but horror. The waves of the magic sea called out in the sunlight: "There must be a God." The demoniac radio answers in the dark: "There can't be." Belief was so easy then; it has grown so hard now; and life, the individual life, that for an awakening child was so boundless, has it drawn into this – this alley-way between tall cypresses that must join somewhere in the mist? But stop, we are getting near No Man's Land again. Turn back.

Moving pictures love to give us nowadays "cavalcades" of events, to mark the flight of time. Each of us carries his own. Mine shows, as its opening, the sea beaches of the Isle of Wight. . . . Then turn on Portchester village and its Roman castle. . . . Queen Victoria going past in a train, in the dark, putting her head out of the window (her eight heads out of eight windows). . . . Now shift to an Atlantic sailing steamer (type of 1876) with people emigrating to Canada. . . . Then a Canadian farm in a lost corner of Ontario up near Lake Simcoe for six years. . . . Put in bears, though there weren't any . . . boarding-school, scenes at Upper Canada College – the real old rough stuff . . . University, cap and gown days, old style; put a long beard on the president; show fourteen boarding-houses at $4.50 a week. . . . School teaching – ten years – (run it fast – I want to forget it). . . .

Then make the film Chicago University with its saloons of forty years ago, a raw place, nowhere to smoke. . . . And then settle the film down to McGill University, and run it round and round as slowly as you like for thirty-six sessions – college calling in the Autumn, students and co-eds and Rah! Rah! all starting afresh, year after year. . . . College in the snow, the February classroom; hush! don't wake them, it's a lecture in archaeology. . . . All of it again and again. . . . College years, one after the other. . . . Throw in, as interludes, journeys to England, a lecture trip around the Empire. . . . Put in Colombo, Ceylon, for atmosphere. . . . Then more college years. . . .

Then loud music and the Great War with the college campus all at drill, the boys of yesterday turned to men. . . . Then the war over, lecture trips to the U.S. . . . Pictures of Iowa State University. . . . Ladies' Fortnightly Club – about forty of them. . . . Then back to the McGill campus. . . . Retirement. . . . An honorary degree ("this venerable scholar"). . . . And then unexpectedly the war again and the Black Watch back on the McGill campus.

Such is my picture, the cavalcade all the way down from the clouds of the morning to the mists of the evening.

As the cavalcade passes down the years it is odd how gradually and imperceptibly the change of outlook comes, from the eyes of wonder to those of disillusionment – or is it to those of truth? A child's world is full of celebrated people, wonderful people like the giants and magicians of the picture books. Later in life the celebrated people are all gone. There aren't any – or not made of what it once meant.

I recall from over half a century ago a prize-day speaker at Upper Canada College telling us that he saw before him the future statesmen, the poets, the generals and the leaders of the nation. I thought the man a nut to say that. What he saw was just us. Yet he turned out to be correct; only in a sense he wasn't; it was still only us after all. It is the atmosphere of illusion that cannot last.

Yet some people, I know, are luckier in this than I am. They're born in a world of glamour and live in it. For them there are great people everywhere, and the illusion seems to feed itself. One such I recall out of the years, with a capacity for admiration all his own.

"I sat next to Professor Buchan at the dinner last night," he once told me. "He certainly is a great scholar, a marvelous philologian!"

"Is he?" I said.

"Yes," my friend continued. "I asked him if he thought the Indian word *snabe* was the same as the German word *knabe*."

"And what did he say?"

"He said he didn't know."

And with that my friend sat back in quiet appreciation of such accurate scholarship and of the privilege of being near it. There are many people like that, decent fellows to be with. Their illusions keep their life warm.

But for most of us they fade out, and life itself as we begin to look back on it appears less and less. Has it all faded to this? There comes to me the story of an old Carolina negro who found himself, after years of expectancy, privileged to cast a vote. After putting the ballot paper in the box he stood, still expectant, waiting for what was to happen, to come next. And then, in disillusionment: "Is that all there is, boss? Is that all there is to it?"

"That's all," said the presiding officer.

So it is with life. The child says "when I am a big boy" – but what is that? The boy says "when I grow up" – and then, grown up, "when I get married." But to be married, once done and over, what is that again? The man says "when I can retire" – and then when retirement comes he looks back over the path traversed, a cold wind sweeps over the fading landscape and he feels somehow that he has missed it all. For the reality of life, we learn too late, is in the living tissue of it from day to day, not in the expectation of better, nor in the fear of worse. Those two things, to be always looking ahead and to worry over things that haven't yet happened and very likely won't happen – those take the very essence out of life.

If one could only live each moment to the full, in a present, intense with its own absorption, even if as transitory and evanescent as Einstein's "here" and "now." It is strange how we cry out in our collective human mind against this restless thinking and clamour for time to stand still – longing for a land where it is always afternoon, or for a book of verses underneath a bough where we may let the world pass.

But perhaps it is this worry, this restlessness, that keeps us on our necessary path of effort and endeavour. Most of us who look back from old age have at least a comfortable feeling that we have "got away with it." At least we kept out of jail, out of the asylum and out of the poor house. Yet one still needs to be careful. Even "grand old men" get fooled sometimes. But at any rate we don't want to start over; no, thank you, it's too hard. When I look back at long evenings of study in boarding-house bedrooms, night after night, one's head sinking at times over the dictionary – I wonder how I did it.

And school days – at Upper Canada College anno Domini 1882 – could I stand that now? If some one asked me to eat "supper" at six and then go and study next day's lessons, in silence in the long study from seven to nine-thirty – how would that be? A school waiter brought round glasses of water on a tray at half-past eight, and if I asked for a whisky and soda could I have had it? I could not. Yet I admit there was the fun of putting a bent pin – you know how, two turns in it – on the seat where the study master sat. And if I were to try that now at convocation they wouldn't understand it. Youth is youth, and age is age.

So many things, I say, that one went through seem hopelessly difficult now. Yet other things, over which youth boggles and hesitates and palpitates, seem so easy and so simple to old age. Take the case of women, I mean girls. Young men in love go snooping around, hoping, fearing, wondering, lifted up at a word, cast down by an eyebrow. But if he only knew enough, any young man – as old men see it – could have any girl he wanted. All he need do is to step up to her and say, "Miss Smith, I don't know you, but your overwhelming beauty forces me to speak; can you marry me at, say, three-thirty this afternoon?"

I mean that kind of thing in that province of life would save years of trepidation. It's just as well, though, that they don't know it or away goes all the pretty world of feathers and flounces, of flowers and dances that love throws like a gossamer tissue across the path of life.

On such a world of youth, old age can only gaze with admiration. As people grow old all youth looks beautiful to them. The plainest girls are pretty with nature's charms. The dullest duds are at least young. But age cannot share it. Age must sit alone.

The very respect that young people feel for the old – or at least for the established, the respectable, by reason of those illusions of which I spoke – makes social unity impossible. An old man may think himself a "hell of a feller" inside, but his outside won't justify it. He must keep to his corner or go "ga-ga," despised of youth and age alike. . . .

In any case, to put it mildly, old men are tiresome company. They can't listen. I notice this around my club. We founded it thirty years ago and the survivors are all there, thirty years older than they were thirty years ago, and some even more, much more. Can they listen? No, not even to me. And when they start to tell a story they ramble on and on, and you know the story anyway because it's the one you told them yesterday. Young people when they talk have to be snappy and must butt in and out of conversation as they get a chance. But once old men are given rope, you have to pay it out to them like a cable. To my mind the only tolerable old men are the ones – you notice lots of them when you look for them – who have had a stroke – not a tragic one; that would sound cruel – but just one good flap of warning. If I want to tell a story, I look round for one of these.

The path through life I have outlined from youth to age, you may trace for yourself by the varying way in which strangers address you. You begin as "little man" and then "little boy," because a little man is littler than a little boy; then "sonny" and then "my boy" and after that "young man" and presently the interlocutor is younger than yourself and says, "Say, mister." I can still recall the thrill of pride I felt when a Pullman porter first called me "doctor" and when another one raised me up to "judge," and then the terrible shock it was when a taxi man swung open his door and said, "Step right in, dad."

It was hard to bear when a newspaper reporter spoke of me as the "old gentleman," and said I was very simply dressed. He was a liar; those were my best things. It was a worse shock when a newspaper first called me a septuagenarian, another cowardly lie, as I was only sixty-nine and seven-twelfths. Presently I shall be introduced as "this venerable old gentleman" and the axe will fall when they raise me to the degree of "grand old man." That means on our continent any one with snow-white hair who has kept out of jail till eighty. That's the last and worst they can do to you.

Yet there is something to be said even here for the mentality of age. Old people grow kinder in their judgment of others. They are able to comprehend, even if not to pardon, the sins and faults of others. If I hear of a man robbing a cash register of the shop where he works, I think I get the idea. He wanted the cash. If I read of a man burning down his store to get the insurance, I see that what he wanted was the insurance. He had nothing against the store. Yet somehow just when I am reflecting on my own kindliness I find myself getting furious with a waiter for forgetting the Worcester sauce.

This is the summary of the matter that as for old age there's nothing to it, for the individual looked at by himself. It can only be reconciled with our view of life insofar as it has something to pass on, the new life of children and of grandchildren, or if not that, at least some recollection of good deeds, or of something done that may give one the hope to say, *non omnis moriar* (I shall not altogether die).

Give me my stick. I'm going out on to No Man's Land. I'll face it.

Index: These Is No Index

Index: There Is No Index

READERS of books, I mean worth-while readers, like those who read this volume, will understand how many difficulties centre round the making of an Index. Whether to have an Index at all? Whether to make it a great big one, or just a cute little Index on one page? Whether to have only proper names, or let it take in ideas – and so so. In short the thing reaches dimensions that may raise it to the rank of being called the Index Problem, if nothing is done about it.

Of course one has to have an Index. Authors themselves would prefer not to have any. Having none would save trouble and compel reviewers to read the whole book instead of just the Index. But the reader needs it. Otherwise he finds himself looking all through the book, forwards and then backwards, and then plunging in at random, in order to read out to a friend what it was that was so darned good about Talleyrand. He doesn't find it, because it was in another book.

So let us agree, there must be an Index. Now comes the trouble. What is the real title or name of a thing or person that has three or four? Must you put everything three or four times over in the Index, under three or four names? No, just once, so it is commonly understood; and then for the other joint names, we put what is called a cross-reference, meaning, "See this" or "See that." It sounds good in theory, but in practice it leads to such results as – *Talleyrand, see Perigord* . . . and when you hunt this up, you find –

Perigord, Bishop of, see Talleyrand. The same effect can be done flat out, with just two words, as *Lincoln, see Abraham . . . Abraham, see Lincoln*. But even that is not so bad because at least it's a closed circle. It comes to a full stop. But compare the effect, familiar to all research students, when the circle is not closed. Thus, instead of just seeing Lincoln, the unclosed circle runs like this, each item being hunted up alphabetically, one after the other – *Abraham, see Lincoln . . . Lincoln, see Civil War . . . Civil War, see United States . . . United States, see America . . . America, see American History . . . American History, see also Christopher Columbus, New England, Pocahontas, George Washington* . . . the thing will finally come to rest somehow or other with the dial point at *see Abraham Lincoln*.

But there is worse even than that. A certain kind of conscientious author enters only proper names, but he indexes them every time they come into his book, no matter how they come in, and how unimportant is the context. Here is the result in the Index under the Letter N:

Napoleon – 17, 26, 41, 73, 109, 110, 156, 213, 270, 380, 460. You begin to look them up. Here are the references:

Page 17 – "wore his hair like Napoleon."
Page 26 – "in the days of Napoleon."
Page 41 – "as fat as Napoleon."
Page 73 – "not so fat as Napoleon."
Page 109 – "was a regular Napoleon at Ping-pong."
Page 110 – "was not a Napoleon at Ping-pong."
Page 156 – "Napoleon's hat."
Pages 213, 270, 380, 460, not investigated.

Equally well meant but perhaps even harder to bear is the peculiar kind of index that appears in a biography. The name of the person under treatment naturally runs through almost every page, and the conscientious index-maker tries to keep pace with him. This means that many events of his life get shifted out of their natural order. Here is the general effect:

John Smith: born.p.1: born again.p.1: father born.p.2: grandfather born.p.3: mother born.p.4: mother's family leave Ireland.p.5: still leaving it.p.6: school.p.7: more school.p.8: dies of pneumonia and enters Harvard.p.9: eldest son born.p.10: marries.p.11: back at school.p.12: dead.p.13: takes his degree.p.14: . . .

Suppose, then, you decide to get away from all these difficulties and make a Perfect Index in which each item shall carry with it an explanation, a sort of little epitome of what is to be found in the book. The reader consulting the volume can open the Index, look at a reference, and decide whether or not he needs to turn the subject up in the full discussion in the book. A really good Index will in most cases itself give the information wanted. There you have, so to speak, the Perfect Index.

Why I know about this is because I am engaged at present in making such an Index in connection with a book on gardening, which I am writing just now. To illustrate what is meant, I may be permitted to quote the opening of the book, and its conversion into Index Material:

As Abraham Lincoln used to say, when you want to do gardening, you've got to take your coat off, a sentiment shared by his fellow enthusiast, the exiled Napoleon, who, after conquering all Europe, retaining only the sovereignty of the spade in his garden plot at St. Helena, longed only for more fertilizer.

As arranged for the Index, the gist, or essential part of this sentence, the nucleus, so to speak, appears thus:

Abraham Lincoln; habit of saying things, p.1; wants to do gardening, p.1; takes his coat off, p.1; his enthusiasm, p.1; compared with Napoleon, p.1.

Coat; taken off by Abraham Lincoln, p. 1.

Gardening; Lincoln's views on, p.1; need of taking coat off, for, p.1; Napoleon's enthusiasm over, p.1; see also under spade, sovereignty, St. Helena.

Napoleon; his exile, p.1; conquers Europe, p.1; enthusiastic over gardening, p.1; compared with Lincoln; retains sovereignty of spade, p.1; plots at St. Helena, p.1; longs for fertilizer, p.1; see also Europe, St. Helena, fertilizer, seed catalogue, etc., etc. . . .

That's as far as I've got with the sentence. I still have to write up *sovereignty, spade, sentiment, share, St. Helena*, and everything after S. There's no doubt it's the right method, but it takes time somehow to get the essential nucleus of the gist, and express it. I see why it is easier to do the other thing. But then sin is always easier than righteousness. See also under Hell, road to, Pavement, and Intentions, good.

L'Envoi: A Salutation Across the Sea

L'Envoi: A Salutation Across the Sea

THE BRITISH are an odd people. They have their own ways and they stick to them; and I like every one of them.

They have their own way of talking. When an Englishman has anything surprising to tell he never exaggerates it, never overstates it – in fact he makes as little of it as possible. And a Scotchman doesn't even mention it. An Englishman can speak of a play of Shakespeare as "rather good," and of grand opera as "not half bad." He can call Haile Selassie a "rather decent little chap," and the President of the United States a "thoroughly good sort."

Sometimes this modesty of speech is perhaps carried a little too far. An Englishman when he has to talk about himself, doesn't refer to himself as "I," but calls himself "one." In my club the other day a newly arrived Englishman said, "One finds Canada simply wonderful; of course one had seen India and all that, but here one finds everything so different." What could I answer except to say that one was terribly glad to know that one liked Canada, that if one would take a drink with one, one would push the bill. Yet I like that way of talking. It's better than the everlasting "I – I – I." Only I think that next time I'll call myself "two."

A Scotchman of course doesn't use "one." He simply calls himself "a body." He's not referring to his soul, before strangers.

But this modest British way of talking without making

things sound too big has the advantage that it keeps the world in its right focus. On our side of the water we get so filled up with admiration with such a sense of the bigness of potentates and magnates, that we feel small ourselves. We wouldn't know how to behave if we met the Negris of Abyssinia or the Magnum of Magnesia. They're all one to the Britisher – Rajahs, and Rams and Sams, he calls them all "Jimmy."

THE BRITISH ARE AN ODD PEOPLE; even in their recreation. They have their own games, and they carry them all round the world with them. When other nations go among natives they bring a whole collection of decrees and ordinances. The Englishman just brings a briar-root pipe and a cricket bag. He opens it and he says: "Now this is cricket and I'll show you johnnies how to play. Ali Baba, you just roll out that coconut matting and, Ibn Swot, you stick in these wickets." Two seasons later Ali Baba is taken "home" to play for Hants against Bucks, or Potts against Crooks – anyway, another quarter million square miles is annexed.

THE BRITISH ARE AN ODD PEOPLE. They are people of high character; and yet they don't have any particular moral code to guide them. They just go by whether anything is "the thing." If it is, you do it; if it's not you don't. Strangers often wonder, for example, why the Opposition in Parliament doesn't make a row about this or that. But the answer is that it would hardly be "the thing." The whole of British government is carried on in that way. A member rises in the House and asks a question on which seems to hang the whole life of the nation. The Parliamentary Under-Secretary for Horticulture answers that ministers know it but won't say it. Then it's not "the thing" to ask any more. In the United States they need a whole constitution of thousands and thousands of words, and they get tangled up in the clauses. The British constitution is just "the thing." Of course, there are no rules to guide private morals. I mean to say one learnt one's catechism when one was young, but as a matter of fact it is rather the thing to forget it.

YES, THE BRITISH ARE AN ODD PEOPLE; they have their own ways in eating and drinking. And I like them. Take their afternoon tea. They have it at the South Pole, and they serve it half way through a naval engagement. And what, after all, more charming than the tea-tray with its white cloth, the silver tea-pot, the delicate cups and the thin bread and butter; and what better excuse for slipping in a real drink, just after? Sometimes I think that's what it's for. Only you must be careful not to get absent-minded, and when your hostess asks, "How do you take yours?" you mustn't answer, "Off the shelf," or "Plenty of soda, please." Or no – it wouldn't matter. She'd understand and give it to you.

OH, YES, THE BRITISH ARE AN ODD PEOPLE – and I like all their odd ways. Well, after all, why not? I mean to say, one was born in Hampshire, Eh, what.

FINIS

Afterword

BY BARBARA NIMMO

NEW LEACOCK VOLUME

My Remarkable Uncle & Other Sketches

This is another of those characteristic mixed volumes of amusing sketches, "funny pieces," and kindly philosophy, which have carried Stephen Leacock's humour around the world. The contents vary all the way from the out-and-out burlesque of the author's famous *Nonsense Novels* to quiet scholarly discussion that reminds us of Professor Leacock's second profession. Indeed some of the sketches make as near an approach to absolute seriousness as their author ever cares to venture. The title piece, *My Remarkable Uncle*, is a little study, direct from life, of a forgotten magnate of the great days of the Manitoba boom of half a century ago. In this, as in many other of the literary studies in this new volume, Dr. Leacock shows an extraordinary power of reviving byc-gone events in such a way as to leave the humour outstanding and the malice all forgotten. Many of the sketches, however, carry the current interest of the world of the moment. The book is not an anthology culled from previous works but an entirely new volume in itself. As such it is likely, especially in these days of stress, to bring the same comfort and to find the same welcome that has attended Stephen Leacock's books for the past thirty years.

Thus Stephen Leacock wrote in the promotional announcement he sent to Dodd, Mead, his New York publisher, for his forthcoming book, *My Remarkable Uncle*. The volume's title essay, a sketch of his uncle Edward Philip Leacock, "known to ever so many people in Winnipeg fifty or sixty years ago as E.P.," is one of Leacock's best, and the most factual of any he ever wrote.

Shortly after the death of Leacock's wife in 1925, I was invited to come to Montreal to attend McGill University (fortunately, I was ready to enter college), and to help make as normal a family life as possible for my Uncle Stephen and his twelve-year-old son. For ten years – until my marriage in 1937 – I spent the winter months in Montreal, earning my B.A. and M.A. in English and later teaching in the English department at McGill. In the summers we departed for Orillia to spend nearly four months on Lake Couchiching. The present Leacock home in Orillia was planned before his wife died, and we moved in from a smaller cottage in 1928. Thus Leacock knew two worlds: his McGill world of the winters and his Orillia world of the summers.

I was in Orillia when my uncle wrote "My Remarkable Uncle" for the *Reader's Digest* series, "The Most Unforgettable Character I Have Ever Met." The essay appeared in July 1939. It was a great joy to hear him read this aloud, full of enthusiasm. His sonorous voice, infectious laughter, and feeling of pathos gave his reading a depth never to be forgotten. Four or five of us were sitting in the living room of his home when he came in with a sheaf of papers in his hand, anxious for us to hear his newly written piece.

Leacock mentions the "Remarkable Uncle" essay in an earlier letter of September 1936: "When I finish my article on *Social Credit* I am going to start a piece called 'My Amazing Uncle,' – about 5000 words on E.P. Very difficult because I can't tell how much voice and mimic counts for in the E.P. stuff. But I mean to do it in my own way. It will be part of a future volume of reminiscences."

In so many of his books of humour, Leacock seemed to turn hitherto unpublished essays – with a wave of a wand – into chapters of related subjects. In writing to Frank Dodd about the "Uncle Book," he enclosed a short piece written since the time when the manuscript had been submitted, "The Mathematics of the Lost Chord." "This can be used," he wrote, "if more words are needed to fit the space planned. My own opinion is that the more words in a 'funny' book the better. People buy them by the pound and look to see if there's enough."

Thus he had in 1942 gathered together some thirty essays to add to the sketch on E.P. to form a new book. We find in the first chapter, "My Remarkable Uncle," "Old Farm and the New Frame," and "The Struggle to Make Us Gentlemen," written in retrospect on his early life in "the typical farm road and village of fifty years ago – a 'social cell' as I believe the sociologist would call us," where "when I was young if you had $10 in the village no one could change it, and $10 would board you for a month." Two years later, when he was working on his unfinished autobiography, *The Boy I Left Behind Me*, the old farm did not fare so well. He pictured it as the most depressing life, shut off from the world of learning until he was saved by being sent to boarding school.

We always think of Leacock's much quoted line from "Gertrude the Governess": "he flung himself from the room, flung himself upon his horse and rode madly off in all directions." Let us peruse a few others from this collection. There is the old farmhouse kitchen stove, where "You regulated the heat you wanted by the distance you sat from it." Or the North American continent, which "is always being swept by waves – crime waves, drink waves, waves of religion, of speculation – till the back-wash of common sense dries it off again." Or the fisherman in his anchored boat, "fast asleep, his hat fallen over his eyes, his line dangling in the water, but with a magazine across his lap to show that his brain made a fight for it." Or the two students who "wrote notes in diligent despair like distressed mariners working to keep a boat afloat."

It is so often said that Leacock was anti-feminist. "Social policy should proceed from the fundamental truth that women are and must be dependent," he wrote in 1915. But in everything he did in his own life, he encouraged women to develop their talents, and he helped them to achieve their ambitions. He had great respect and admiration for his sister Rosamond, who was one of the first women physicians in Canada; she had attended McGill University, the University of Toronto, and then the Johns Hopkins University. And he was so helpful to many of my friends and other women students, showing great interest in their careers. He was quick to write letters of recommendation and to offer them sincere encouragement. In September 1940, he wrote to the daughter of one of his friends, "Remember if one thing fails, the next one doesn't and that for people who have brains and energy and youth, the world is *still* wide open."

Leacock's Christmas tales tell a great deal about him. There was a certain shyness in his character – not completely sure about himself – an inadequacy about expressing his feelings towards people. He did not know how to enter into festivities wholeheartedly. Though not a melancholy person, he felt a certain sadness during his last twenty years when faced with the gaiety of Christmas. He tried to make it a festive time for his young son by opening up the country home in Orillia, yet a feeling of sadness prevailed.

One essay to which I would particularly like to add an afterword is "The Passing of the Kitchen." Once again a group of us were sitting around in the Orillia living room. As a new bride, I said something about having had a dinner party. I had no maid, as my uncle observed, and so how could I have had a dinner party? Uncle Stephen was quick to turn my answer into a description of the new maidless household, where "the charming little hostess, who has just served the cocktails, dainty as if she never worked a minute in her life, and cool as a lobster salad. She just turns on a 'control' to keep its eye on the roast, sets the soupometer for seventy degrees, turns on enough electric heat to freeze the cocktail, and there you are!"

An interesting note accompanied the final essay, "L'Envoi: A Salutation Across the Sea," when it was submitted to a newspaper or magazine. There is no date and no address.

> Dear Mr. Smith-Ross,
>
> In accordance with correspondence with Mr. J.K. Thomas I send you the enclosed. I hope it is what you want. I am sure it is.
>
> If you can use it label it as you like, – *Things British* or without any title . . . just start out: – STEPHEN LEACOCK in a delightful discussion of national characteristics, says: [here follows the essay].

For one who knew Stephen Leacock, the essays of *My Remarkable Uncle* touch on so many of the things he enjoyed in life. He forever loved fishing, which was very much part of his life. In Orillia he had fishing rights on an excellent farm trout stream, which he stocked with trout several different summers. Then there was bass fishing on Lake Couchiching and on Lake Simcoe. And he loved preparing for an outing, collecting the bait, arranging the picnic lunch, all of this carried out with great enthusiasm, which made the occasion exciting for us all. Who else would have thought to dub a picnic "Eating Air"?

In "Three Score and Ten," Leacock once again dwells on "The Business of Growing Old." He runs through a "cavalcade" of events in his life, "all the way down from the clouds of the morning to the mists of the evening." For him, "the reality of life . . . is in the living tissue of it from day to day, not in the expectation of better, nor in the fear of worse."

"Age must sit alone," Leacock concludes, and this mood persisted with him the last few years of his life. His son was working in Toronto. I was married and living in Detroit. Many of his friends had died. The war hung heavily over his mind. His writing, fortunately, kept him going.

BY STEPHEN LEACOCK

AUTOBIOGRAPHY

The Boy I Left Behind Me (1946)

BIOGRAPHY

Mark Twain (1932)

Charles Dickens: His Life and Work (1933)

DRAMA

"Q": A Farce in One Act [with Basil Macdonald] (1915)

ECONOMICS

Economic Prosperity in the British Empire (1930)

Back to Prosperity: The Great Opportunity of the Empire Conference (1932)

The Gathering Financial Crisis in Canada: A Survey of the Present Critical Situation (1936)

EDUCATION

The Pursuit of Knowledge: A Discussion of Freedom and Compulsion in Education (1934)

Too Much College, or Education Eating Up Life (1939)

HISTORY

Baldwin, Lafontaine, Hincks: Responsible Government (1907)

Adventures of the Far North:
A Chronicle of the Frozen Seas (1914)
The Dawn of Canadian History: A Chronicle of Aboriginal Canada and the Coming of the White Man (1914)
The Mariner of St. Malo:
A Chronicle of the Voyages of Jacques Cartier (1914)
Mackenzie, Baldwin, Lafontaine, Hincks (1926)
Lincoln Frees the Slaves (1934)
The British Empire:
Its Structure, Its History, Its Strength (1940)
Canada: The Foundations of Its Future (1941)
Our Heritage of Liberty: Its Origin, Its Achievement, Its Crisis: A Book for War Time (1942)
Montreal: Seaport and City (1942)
Canada and the Sea (1944)

HUMOUR

Literary Lapses (1910)
Nonsense Novels (1911)
Sunshine Sketches of a Little Town (1912)
Behind the Beyond, and Other Contributions to Human Knowledge (1913)
Arcadian Adventures with the Idle Rich (1914)
Moonbeams from the Larger Lunacy (1915)
Further Foolishness:
Sketches and Satires on the Follies of the Day (1916)
Frenzied Fiction (1918)
The Hohenzollerns in America: with the Bolsheviks in Berlin, and Other Impossibilities (1919)
Winsome Winnie, and Other New Nonsense Novels (1920)
My Discovery of England (1922)
College Days (1923)
Over the Footlights (1923)
The Garden of Folly (1924)
Winnowed Wisdom: A New Book of Humour (1926)
Short Circuits (1928)

The Iron Man and the Tin Woman, with Other Such Futurities (1929)
Wet Wit and Dry Humour: Distilled from the Pages of Stephen Leacock (1931)
The Dry Pickwick and Other Incongruities (1932)
Afternoons in Utopia: Tales of the New Time (1932)
Hellements of Hickonomics in Hiccoughs of Verse Done in Our Social Planning Mill (1936)
Funny Pieces: A Book of Random Sketches (1936)
Here Are My Lectures (1937)
Model Memoirs, and Other Sketches from Simple to Serious (1938)
My Remarkable Uncle, and Other Sketches (1942)
Happy Stories, Just to Laugh At (1943)
Last Leaves (1945)

LITERARY CRITICISM

Essays and Literary Studies (1916)
Humour: Its Theory and Technique (1935)
The Greatest Pages of American Humor (1936)
Humour and Humanity: An Introduction to the Study of Humour (1937)
How to Write (1943)

POLITICAL SCIENCE

Elements of Political Science (1906)
The Unsolved Riddle of Social Justice (1920)
My Discovery of the West: A Discussion of East and West in Canada (1937)
While There Is Time: The Case against Social Catastrophe (1945)

TITLES BY STEPHEN LEACOCK
Available in the New Canadian Library

LITERARY LAPSES with an afterword by Robertson Davies
7710-99835 $4.95 ☐

SUNSHINE SKETCHES OF A LITTLE TOWN with an afterword by Jack Hodgins
7710-99843 $5.95 ☐

ARCADIAN ADVENTURES WITH THE IDLE RICH with an afterword by Gerald Lynch
7710-99665 $5.95 ☐

MOONBEAMS FROM THE LARGER LUNACY
7710-91435 $4.95 ☐

WINNOWED WISDOM
7710-91745 $4.95 ☐

MY REMARKABLE UNCLE with an afterword by Barbara Nimmo
7710-9965-7 $5.95 ☐

LAST LEAVES
7710-91699 $5.95 ☐

BUY THESE QUALITY BOOKS AT YOUR LOCAL BOOKSTORE OR USE THIS CONVENIENT COUPON FOR ORDERING.

NEW CANADIAN LIBRARY McClelland & Stewart Inc.
25 Hollinger Road, Toronto, Ontario M4B 3G2

Please send me the book(s) I have checked above. I am enclosing a cheque or money order for a total of $ ______________
(no cash or C.O.D.s please). Or, please charge my
Visa account # ______________________ ,expiry date ________.
Please add $1.50 to your first book to cover postage and handling, and an additional 75 cents for each additional book you order.

Name ______________________________________

Address __________________________ Apt. __________

City ______________________________________

Province _______________________ Postal Code __________

Please make your cheque payable to McClelland & Stewart Inc. and allow 4 to 6 weeks for delivery. Prices and availability subject to change without notice.